Prelude to Ballet:

a soviet girl who dances and dreams

by Ganna Onipko

COVER DESIGN by Nicholas J. Adames and Jimmy Adames

ISBN: 9781726840217

FIRST EDITION

For my Parents -
whose permanent love and hopefulness
have guided me through

TABLE OF CONTENTS

Author in traditional Soviet era school Uniform, 1984

Chapter 1: RETURN

"Hurry up and finish your tea, I need the glasses before we reach the city limits." A train conductor with messy hair and overslept eyes pulls the door of our coupe wide open. "And don't forget to take the sheets off the beds and bring them to me too."

I try to gulp the rest of the tea from the thin glass placed inside of a metal cup with a handle, a traditional serving gear in all the long distance trains of the Soviet Union. Choking on the hot liquid, I'm already up on my feet helping Babushka with bedding.

My life is full of orders coming from my parents, from my strict Babushka, and of course from the teachers at the academy. "Academy" – it's been so long since I've crossed its lobby and said "Hello" to the concierge. Our leaving the city was such a sudden event; it felt more like escape. That night before I left, Papa spent a long time on the phone digging for bits of truth about the real threat that the explosion in the nuclear power plant called Chernobyl caused our city and its inhabitants. I went to bed as usual: with my school uniform ready for the next morning, my ballet slippers washed and ribbons carefully ironed. I never expected to be woken up before dawn and handed a suitcase. Then, I was taken to the train station, while staring from the car's window at the people on the dark streets oddly dressed in white overalls with faces hidden behind masks. They were washing the city, pouring water from the fire hoses on the trees, the facades of the houses, and the sidewalks. They tried to get rid of the radiation – an invisible threat formed of the tiniest particles that didn't have any smell or taste, yet blown by the wind from the site of the exploded nuclear reactor. The water packed with those dangerous radioactive particles ran down the streets, into the sewer, and all the way into our beautiful river Dnieper, where the drinking water supply came from. Remembering that day and how horrifying it felt to leave behind my parents tightens a knot in my throat.

"Miroslava, would you stop dreaming and get moving, we should arrive to Kiev in twenty minutes or less." Babushka's voice rescues me from my memories.

"Do you think they'll bring Niko?" Babushka ignores my question while my impatience to see my parents and my dog grows with every second. We've never been apart for so long. My beautiful Russian hound seems taller every time I spend a long weekend away. How different will I find him now, after being away for the long four months?

I watch the Kiev suburbs flicker behind the window. Babushka tosses undressed pillows into the upper beds of our four people occupancy coupe; to our unprecedented luck we've been traveling alone. She passes me a heavy bunch of grayish sheets and I rush to the maintenance room to get rid of them.

By now, the train enters the city and is rolling across the high bridge of a half a mile-wide river.

Instead of getting back to our coupe, I stop next to its door, in the narrow hallway of the train's car, and look out the window. I never get tired of the view that opens from the bridge: the tall hills of the western bank of the Dnieper River are covered with a thick rug of dense trees. Over the tree tops, rise the magnificent churches of white brick topped with multiple golden onions for the roofs. Proud to be born in such beautiful city, also a capital of the Soviet Republic of Ukraine, I admire the breathtaking sight of the churches and cathedrals while trying to ignore the structure on the opposite side from the golden tops. The gigantic statue of the Mother of the Motherland, or the "Iron Lady" as people call it, holds a sword in one hand and a shield in the other. It has been mounted in memory of World War II and symbolizes a protection from the outside enemies that unbeatable Soviet Union offers to its citizens. I grin, remembering how as a child instead of feeling protected, I felt frightened by the steel figure with the woman-like body yet masculine face. However, the orthodox cathedrals with glorious golden crosses always brought me a sense of peace and protection.

The scenery flashing past the window is an architectural mixture. There are soviet-built box-like structures with multiple holes for windows and tiny balconies; they look embarrassed next to the elegant buildings of the 19th century with arched windows and columns embellished by moldings and numerous small statues. When Babushka joins me by the window, I think she can hear my heart pounding in excitement and anticipation: the train bringing me home is about to arrive.

Chapter 2: BIG CHANGES

Squeezed between Babushka and Niko in the back of our small car, I feel my head spinning from excitement of being back with my parents and from the lack of fresh air.

"Mama, is Natasha back? Where do you think she spent her summer? Have you gone back to our dacha, Papa? Can I get a new school bag for this year?" I overflow with questions that keep spilling out in an unstoppable waterfall.

"Natasha is back. Her mom called yesterday. She told me that Marina Ivanovna was fired. So, all of you girls must prepare for a change."

It is sauna hot in the car, yet suddenly my face feels icy cold. The sound of the big city coming from the open windows interferes with Mama's quiet voice, and for a second I'm hoping I heard her wrong.

"Marina Ivanovna didn't show up at work when all of her ballet students, except for you, were still in class," continues Mama. "She was fired for deserting her students."

"But it's not fair, everyone was ordered to leave just a few days later!"

"Well, everyone followed the official orders and she didn't. I went through the trouble of getting that fake note from our physician for you," Papa joins in the conversation, "Yet, they still sent that senseless letter of your expulsion, remember?"

"I was expelled? I don't remember any letter!"

"You can't remember because I didn't tell you," Mama quickly interrupts. "You felt miserable and scared enough because of our sudden separation, so I hid the letter away, planning to deal with it later. When a few weeks passed and most children were finally evacuated from the city following government's order, the second letter arrived. It stated that expulsion was a mistake. Now, forget about it, I don't even know why your father brought it up." I hear annoyance and irritability in Mama's voice. She also gives Papa a look, and although I can't see the expression on her face, I picture it well. Mama is the only one in the family who guards my feelings like a hawk; sometime it appears to me that she shields me too much from the real world.

The car makes a sharp turn and begins to climb a hilly street. I peer out the window at my dear neighborhood: I often walk this street on my way to the subway station and know every dip and every crack in its pavement. The windows and balconies of the five-story apartment buildings along the street hide behind the dense fruit trees. The contrast between the trees and their trunks, painted in vibrant white, reminds me of the spring. It catches my eye as something unusual: the leaves on the trees and the grass beneath are still surprisingly green.

"Why are the trees so green? I always remember lots of yellow by the time school resumes and how sad I feel to say farewell to summer. Does that mystic radiation actually preserve the color?"

"Radiation doesn't preserve anything, it just kills." Papa drives into the wide sidewalk to park next to the door that leads to the common lobby of our apartment building. "The radioactive contaminants released into atmosphere during and after Chernobyl explosion exceeded the Hiroshima nuclear bomb explosion by three hundred times. Everything was contaminated with radioactive particles, and the only way to get rid of them quickly was to keep pouring water on the city all summer long. The immense amount of water is what kept vegetation so green, not deadly radiation."

"Okay, Professor Techenko, that's enough of nuclear physics and history lessons combined. Dochen'ka[1], welcome home." Mama looks at me over her shoulder and I notice a new wrinkle making it way between her eyebrows. "Unfortunately, *Radiation* is a part of our life now, you'll see it soon."

I run the stairs all the way up to the third floor and burst into our apartment. I find my room sparkly clean and also very empty without the stuffed toys and potted plants on the shelves.

"They gather too much dust," explains Mama when she catches my questioning stare. She pulls a floral curtain over my wide window to block the midday sun; then walks out of the room. I hear her lighten the gas flame in the water boiler in the kitchen. I open each drawer in my wardrobe, checking on my belongings that

---

[1] An affectionate word for daughter.

I left behind so suddenly. The top one holds all my ballet class attire: two tank leotards, one light blue, the other one black, two matching elastic belts and two pairs of tights. By one glance, I know the tights won't fit me anymore. What do I wear for the first ballet class? The uniform supply place doesn't open until the first day of school. I decide to try the tights anyway; with my best effort I pull them from my ankles to the knees, and then all the way up. When they reach to my waist, the fabric is so stretched – it's about to rip. My legs stiffen and I can't even *Plié* when I try. Frustrated, I pull off the tights, sit on my bed and complain to my dog.

"Great, I might have to wear the socks on my bare legs for my first ballet class with a new teacher. That would be a remarkable first day of school for your sister, Niko." The dog's eyes are fixed on me; his body is as still as my narrow bed which he lays next to, yet his eyebrows are moving up and down. I chuckle and feel relieved. Not having any other siblings, I find myself talking to my dog a lot and to the trees outside of the window. I remember these massive poplars since I was a little girl; they always peeked through the curtains during the day; their lullaby rustling coming into a wide open fortochka[2] helped me fall asleep. I whisper "Hello" to the trees, noticing that birds are missing. The pigeons, the sparrows and the crows - the loud feathery gang is nowhere to be seen. They must have left the city with the children. Only the children have returned. I glance at the widespread courtyard and spot a few youngsters mooching about on the playground, looking bored; a group of babushkas on the benches busy rumoring. Everything and everyone seem exactly the way I left them. Yet, I recall my parents' concerned preaching in the car about the big changes and also about the post-Chernobyl "diet". Suddenly I feel hungry and head towards the kitchen, Niko follows.

I find Mama standing over the stove making her coffee in the tiny copper pot and watching it not to overflow.

"Mamochka[3], is there anything to eat? I'm a little hungry."

---

[2] A small opening window pane.
[3] An affectionate word for Mama.

"I don't have anything cooked yet, but look in the fridge and the pantry for a quick snack."

I open the refrigerator but find it very empty. Yet the pantry shelves are packed with cardboard boxes and cans.

"What are all of these?"

"It's our new food supply, you know, like for the cosmonauts: pate from tubes and milk from powder."

Mama chuckles but I don't feel amused. I'm determined to find something real. A simple glass of milk will do. Yet, I end up mixing a white powder that smells nothing like milk with triple-boiled water. It tastes worse than it smells.

Papa returns from taking Babushka to her apartment. He joins Mama and me at the table: my parents are drinking their black coffee as I am suffering over the milk and buckwheat flour pancakes.

"Kitten, you'll get used to it. And then, it's not going to be forever, right Pavel?"

"Hopefully not. Winter should bring lots of snow and it'll clear the ground from most of the radioactive remnants when it thaws in the spring."

I sigh, imagining how incredibly far away spring is and how much patience and strength it will take to get us through the long winter.

Later that evening, I lay down in my own bed, trying to picture getting back to the routine at the Academy in just two days. I missed our ballet classes with an intense *Barre* work followed by the challenging and often exhausting *Pas*[4] in the *Center*. I also will be glad to see my regular curriculum teachers and even look forward to learning functions in math and verb conjugations in Russian language. But most of all, I'm impatient to see Natasha and my other Academy friends. A mix of emotions arises and keeps me awake. The questions keep popping in my head: what will be the new teacher like? Will the rest of the girls in my class look as grown and as out of shape as I do? What if the winter turns out to be snowless and we'll be stuck with contaminated fruits and vegetables for the rest of the year? Finally, worn out by my troubling thoughts, I drift into an anxious sleep.

---

[4] Various ballet steps

Chapter 3: "AMAZING FOUR"

Today is the first of September, the day when the children from the fifteen republics of Soviet Union start back to school; all on this same day despite the different languages and distinguished traditions, yet united under the common government into one enormous country.

"Mamochka, please help me put my hair into the bun, it just won't obey my hands today."

I hear Papa opening front door, bringing Niko from his morning walk. "It's time to go Mira!"

I hate to be rushed, especially on such an important day, but he is right – we still need to stop by the market and get flowers; it's a long time tradition to greet teachers with a bouquet on the first day of school. Mama hands me my school bag and I wrap my hands around her. For a moment, I feel so vulnerable and can't imagine letting go.

"Can't be late, kitten, you must leave now. Remember, you are not ten years old and just starting the Academy anymore. It's your third year already. No little girl worries – you know what to expect and how to handle it. You are my "Brave Tin Soldier."

Mama gives me a kiss and off we go, walking down the street towards the market. The city looks like a mobile garden: the vibrant colors of the fall flowers brighten my spirit. There are asters, dahlias, gladioluses, and my all-time favorite - chrysanthemums. While at the market, I quickly choose three colorful bunches that barely fit in my hands. Papa takes off towards the bus stop and I trot in the direction of the tram.

When I get to the tram stop, I see other school children waiting there. Suddenly I realize I'm not wearing my red Pioneer scarf like the rest of them. A tremor rushes through my body. If I return to the apartment for the scarf, I could be late for school. I hesitate for a moment, considering a possibility to avoid the Principal and his assistant for the entire day. Not a chance; not when we all have to line up in the open courtyard before school starts. I race back to the apartment and then back to the tram. I see its yellow and red cart coming and realize I won't be late after all. Yet, I can't help feel nervous: what bad luck to start the school year forgetting something so important!

After a ten minutes ride (I'm the lucky one who lives very close to the Academy; some of my classmates must commute all the way from across the city), I get off and wait to see if any of my friends arrive from the opposite side. My heart thumps with joy when I see Tanya and Vera crossing the rails. They notice me too and try to wave with their hands full with flowers. We charge towards each other and embrace, beautiful bouquets abandoned on the pavement. A warm friendship hug instantly melts the ice of my nervousness.

"You look so tan – amazing! Have you been to the sea?" Tanya looks at me with admiration.

"I'm so worn out from traveling. My parents dragged me all over the country on their tour. All the way to Lithonia!" Vera pretends to be annoyed but it's obvious she can't wait to tell us about her adventures.

"No way! That far! It's incredible!" I can't help but notice Vera's new school bag. Unconsciously I push mine, with its broken handle that was sewn by Mama last night, behind my back.

We walk towards the school courtyard talking all at the same time and interrupting each other. Natasha separates from the crowd already gathered in front of the Academy's building and dashes towards us. Her beautiful blond curls catch and reflect the sun. I notice her eyes are slightly moist, which makes them look even bigger.

"I'm so happy to see you all, I'm crying!" She is always extra dramatic. I often feel she acts her emotions but it suits her well.

"Finally, the "Amazing Four" are together again!" exclaims Tanya.

Natasha and I felt a special connection since the first weeks at the Academy. And then, last year we became friends with Tanya and Vera. At that time, I was reading Dumas's "Three Musketeers" and while admiring their friendship I once called us "Amazing Four". The name stuck.

"Together in good and against the bad! All for one and one for all!" Laughing, we stack our hands in a pyramid and then throw them up in the air.

Already in front of the Academy's grey building, we hurry to find the rest of our classmates and stand next to them. Everyone looks neat and clean: the white aprons of the girls and white buttoned shirts of the boys turn an already sunny morning into an even brighter one. This is the only day, in addition to few other patriotic holidays, when I consider the boys looking handsome.

After what seems like never ending speeches from several school officials, the tallest boy from the senior class picks up and settles on his shoulder the tiniest freshmen girl. You must be ten at the time you are accepted to the Academy and after eight years of study, you graduate at the age of eighteen. All this time you are referred to as a ballet student and not a dancer, until the graduation day, when you finally get a professional ballet dancer diploma in your hands and ready to join a ballet troupe. The senior walks around the perimeter of the courtyard, while the girl on his shoulder ecstatically shakes the big bell in her hand. The court yard fills with the first school bell of the year and everyone cheers.

I join the flow of the students, which carries me and three of my friends into the lobby. We pass the mean, even on this happy day, concierge and continue to the second floor to check the school board. The schedule of the first day is always a surprise.

"We have math first and then geography!" exclaims Tanya being first to fight her way closer to the schedule.

"Classica is right before lunch." I share my discovery. *Classica* is what we call the Classical Ballet Technique class, the most important discipline in our Academy.

"That's superb! We'll have a break right after and lots of time to chat!" cheers Natasha.

Loudly chattering, we head to the math classroom. Tanya gets in first and slides her bag across the last row of desks to secure three more seats for us, which we happily rush into. Max appears in the door's threshold, surrounded by two of his best buddies, his servants and his pleasers, if you ask me. I notice how much taller Max grew over the summer. His black wavy hair falls to his shoulders, adding to his age and making him look even more confident. I hope he will be forced to cut that mane after his first appearance in the Ballet class. The impression in his eyes is boldly clear – he is displeased and annoyed about the "Amazing Four" beating his gang to the "best seats in the house". He hesitates to take what is left, till Marina Stepanovna's plump body pushes him through the door and her commander's voice directs him to the last seat in the first row.

The lesson begins. We all agree on liking math, in fact, it's our second favorite subject after Russian literature. Two years ago, Marina Stepanovna managed to infect us with an odd love for numbers and numerical operations. And here we are, future ballet dancers, who at the most will use math after graduating and joining the ballet troupe for counting ribbons to be cut and sewn onto the point shoes, all excitedly staring at the black board.

While Stepanovna is reviewing last year's material, I observe and assess the rest of my classmates from the excellent view in the back. Slavik is seated next to Max, and the difference between their heights is striking. Slavik looks really small, even vulnerable. I shift my gaze to Larissa, who stares at the black board seemingly struggling to see the numbers. I remember her complaining about her vision at the end of the last year. I thought her deteriorating vision was an outcome of her habit to draw, always and everywhere; even in the dimness of our changing room. Yet, she still didn't get glasses. Larissa appears to have grown as much as I did, but looks extremely thin with skin as white as the snow. Whatever place she spent her summer at, it seriously lacked the sun. I notice Vita who points out the mistake her friend Lena made in solving the equation. Vita reaches for her eraser, passing it to Lena. The girls are an inseparable couple; even though they come from different cities and live at the Academy's dormitory. At the beginning of the school year, they inevitably yearn for their homes and families and need lots of cheering up and support from us, city children.

The rest of the morning passes quickly. After geography everyone scurries down the stairs and into the basement where the changing rooms are.

"Here it is. Welcome to our very own and long desired "Razdevalka[5]!" Vera enters the room first and welcomes the rest of us.

"At last, it's all the way in the back, with no other grades walking through!" I cheer. "We can change, eat, gossip and occasionally take naps with no outsiders' disruption." I try to stretch out on the narrow bench between the shelves enacting the future naps, yet instantly roll down on the floor. My friends giggle.

"Girls, girls look in here! They finally refurbished the showers!" Vita calls from inside the adjunct room with tiled floors and four shower stalls.

"I wonder how long it will be before we have another flood?" remarks Lena.

---

[5] A locker room.

“Should we leave our bags in the lockers with no locks yet installed?” Natasha questions as we change for our ballet class.

“I’m nervous to leave mine for the time we are in *Classica*.” Vera hugs her new bag.

I can relate to her concern. While pulling on my light-blue leotard, I recall my almost new lycra one which disappeared from the changing room last year. I must ask Papa to come right away to install the lock. There is scarce supply of almost everything in the country and anything could be stolen.

With robes slipped over our ballet uniforms, a group of fourteen girls heads towards the dance gallery: a long corridor with large windows looking out to the garden on one side and with seven doors that lead to seven ballet studios on the other. My heart melts when my ear catches the lovely sound of the piano. Our accompanist Leonid is warming up on the baby grand.

Inside the studio, Natasha and I take two large watering cans and fill them with enough water to last throughout the entire class. Then we walk along three walls, wetting the floor next to the ballet *Barres*. There is no more chattering; the time seems to stall and the air fills up with anticipation and fear of unknown. Everyone is peering at the door, waiting to meet the new ballet teacher. And then she appears in the doorway: very tall and straight, her short brown hair and bangs frame her face; her distinguished mouth is alight with scarlet lipstick. Violeta Yurievna enters the studio and terror crawls right beside her.

Chapter 4: VIOLETA

"I look taller, tanner and fatter than any of the girls in my class," I tell Mama that evening as three of us sit down to eat dinner. My nose twitches in dislike as I glance at the food on my plate. Mama frowns. I hurriedly reach for the fork and begin picking at the rice.

"That's your estimate of how you looked and performed in class; you are always so critical about yourself. Besides, after four months break it's normal to feel out of shape. Did Ivetta Yurievna comment on your technique?" Mama elegantly cuts a pickle in half. Even at our simple kitchen table, she looks like she is dining with a queen.

"Her name is Violeta, and yes, from the beginning of the class she clearly showed her disapproval of everything I am and everything I do. She even criticized my tan!" I choke on the rice and vigorously start coughing.

Papa hands me a glass of water and gently pats me on the back.

"My feet weren't obeying during the fast pace of *frappes*, which Violeta made us repeat over and over, asking Leonid to speed up the music with every repetition. Then my feet just went numb and Violeta compared them to the paws of a Bearded Collie: fluffy and soft. With all my love for dogs – I hate that comparison!" Now some rice flies out of my mouth.

"Not sure about Bearded Collie's paws, but now you act like a rude camel!" Papa loses his patience. He never gets too involved with Mama and me talking "ballet". All the details of the ballet class and its French terminology sound foreign to him. He is obviously annoyed by the topic we chose to discuss over dinner.

Yet, my nagging is far from finished. "At the end of the *barre,* during its last exercise everyone struggled to throw their legs high in the air and to make our *grand battements* look light and effortless; we all breathed like a herd of exhausted horses. It's obvious that after the summer all of the girls are out of shape, yet, again, Violeta only shook her head when she passed next to me."

"I'm sure you are exaggerating some. Here, would you like some more sea weed salad?" Mama spoons the dark green strands onto her plate, and then offers the rest to me.

"No thanks." I glance over the food spread on the table; everything's pickled – pickled tomatoes and cucumbers, pickled apples, even a pickled watermelon, "I cannot wait to eat some fresh veggies."

Papa ignores my last comment and returns to the new teacher topic.

"Miroslava, don't jump to negative conclusions yet. Since the first grade at the regular school you've always earned all of your teachers' endorsement. I'm sure Vineta will soon change her attitude too."

"It's Violeta, not Vineta, but Papa is right, she'll notice your natural musicality and stage presence, and what a hard working student you are. Things will improve, you'll see. It's only the first day." Mama grants me a reassuring smile and gently strokes my hair.

We finish the rest of our modest dinner in silence.

I take my parents advice and nourish a hope for positive change; patiently, day after day, I wait for Violeta to warm towards me. But over the next three weeks things do not improve, they worsen during *Classica*.

Today Violeta seems to ignore me in class. In different circumstances lack of attention is considered bad, yet I take it as a blessing. We have completed *barre* and *center* and now are working on *allegro*, which takes place during the last half an hour of the two-hour class. We progress from the small, simple jumps in place to more complex combinations that connect three or more different movements and flow across the studio floor in various patterns. Violeta splits us up in four small groups with only Larissa and me in ours. Being as tall but losing weight seemingly every day, Larissa makes me look heavier.

"Come back to the center, Techenko, and repeat your *grand jete*." Violeta settles on the bench right across from where I stand, with her arms crossed on her chest; her dark brown eyes seem to peer through my skin.

I obey and take a light *glissade* to give myself a strong forward thrust; I put all the power into my left foot and spring up with my right leg thrown high into the air. I land on one leg in *arabesque* with my other leg at a nearly perfect right angle.

"You land the jump as a circus elephant. It was thunder-like loud."

I do it again and this time I put less effort into creating a split in the air but try to land as quiet as possible.

"It looked nothing like *grand jete*. Do you think a jump over a water puddle would do in your Third Level Ballet? Do it again Techenko. And this time put more effort into it. Look, you make the entire class wait."

Without raising my eyes, I feel surrounded by silent pity and compassion, which somehow angers me. Again, I take a preparation, with my head turned towards the mirror and realize I can't stand watching myself. There is not a drop of confidence left in me. Even before I make another attempt to please Violeta, I know it's never going to be good enough.

The class is finally over: however, while I seize my robe from the pile in the corner and then hurry to Razdevalka, I feel no relief but embarrassment to face my classmates.

"As soon as I saw her wearing that black turtleneck, I knew she planned to torture one of us today. Don't you girls notice the connection between her mood and what she wears?" In the comfort of Razdevalka, Natasha unwraps her fancy sandwich. Where does her mom get their food? I wonder while inhaling the smell of salami. It's probably coming from her dad with his government attachments; he has access to the special stores.

"I noticed it too. There are only four colors in Violeta's wardrobe and the most benevolent is beige."

Tanya breaks her canned pork sandwich in half and offers it to Vita. I envy white bread, which has been banned from my diet.

"Yes, it is. And navy is the one that makes her endlessly lecture us on how ballet dancers must forget about anything that normal people do or like," Vera joins in the conversation.

"Although I'm still not sure if it's the clothing which she wears that puts her in the "Mood" or if she wakes up feeling like getting at us and that decides her color selection." I stare inside my lunch sack. Even with Mama trying her best to diversify what I take to school, it's usually pretty much the same – canned pork or sardines on dark wheat bread. I give half to Lena; all of us city kids share our lunches with the dormitory girls. The food served in the Academy's cafeteria tastes disgusting except for the bread, which as dancers we try to avoid.

"And then her theory about feeding on the air. I wonder what she feeds her husband?"

"I bet he is the one cooking. Have you seen her nails?" Natasha stretches out her long fingers, moving them in the same manner that insidious Baba Yaga[6] from the Russian fairy-tales scares little children in the movies.

"I actually felt her nails," says Lena with a sigh. "Check out my back."

We all gather around Lena gasping at the look of her shoulders: multiple red swollen lines cross her skin.

"Have you told your parents?" I demand, feeling resentment overfilling my heart.

"No, it just happened yesterday when Violeta kept correcting my posture pocking underneath my shoulder blades. I'm scheduled to call my mom tomorrow. Still, I'm not going to tell her. It's not like she can change anything or help me not to feel the pain. Why worry her?"

"She is monstrous!" now Vera sounds furious, "Getting at the kids who have no parents to protect them!"

"At least she compliments you a lot too. She tortures, then she praises; she does it to everyone, except

---

[6] A supernatural being of Slavic folklore who appears as a ferocious-looking witch.

for me and Larissa. She never gets at Larissa and I'd take Violeta's nails any day instead of the humiliation she put me through today."

"Larissa, is she your secret relative or something?" asks Tanya and everyone looks in the direction of the pale figure sitting by the window.

The whole time Larissa has been silent, not engaged in our chattering. Sitting on the perch with her sketch pad, gazing out the window, she occasionally moves her pencil over the pad. She catches Tanya's comment though and looks offended. Suddenly her big dark eyes fill with tears.

"We are just kidding. Gosh, you are so sensitive!" exclaims Vera.

"If Violeta treated you the way she treats Mira, there would be enough water to fill up a watering can for the class." Tanya is merciless.

I can't help feeling annoyed about Larissa's perfect form and shape. Lately, we've constantly been compared in class. Thus my friends' support sounds pleasant to my ears. It's Larissa's fault that she stands next to me during *center* practices and makes me hate watching myself in the mirror, which is such an important part of the class: observing and self-correcting.

Everyone finishes their lunches in silence. Larissa is still on the perch; she looks away from us, but in the established quietness, I distinguish her weak sobbing. For a brief moment, there is a fight between good-natured me and the selfish one. It's really not Larissa's fault that Violeta chose me as her victim. I set my sandwich on the bench and walk towards the girl. I sit next to Larissa and hug her scrawny body. Suddenly her head plunges onto my shoulder and we stay that way for a while, weeping together.

Violeta is late for the afternoon *practica,* our two to three hours dance practice during which we learn the variations from the traditional ballets or original choreography. When she finally enters the studio, she holds a folded piece of paper in her hand. She orders all of us to line up in the middle and reads the names of the four girls chosen to be the first cast for "The Jig"; a dance that features four couples and will be performed at the Academy's semiannual performance on the prestigious stage of the city Opera House. I stare at Natasha, surrounded by Vita, Lena and Sveta - all lucky to get a part, and try to justify her being chosen. She does have a very pretty and slender body, and her highly arched feet look so much better in point shoes than mine. Yet, Violeta points out repeatedly to how lazy my friend is. Natasha approaches the corner next to the piano where I hide, trying to control my emotions.

"I'm so happy for you," I whisper, forcing a smile.

"You should be my understudy. You learn choreography faster. This character style dance doesn't really excite me much. It's not even *en pointe.*"

My disappointment triples: not even *en pointe!* If Violeta wasn't the one choosing the cast, how did I not get the part, which calls for so much personality and stage presence? The unavoidable question of the connection between Natasha's dad's government position and her getting a part pops up in my head and sticks around till the end of the day.

That evening, when Mama slides into my room for a good night kiss, I try my best not to sound as distressed as I feel. I recall Lena and the painful looking imprints on her back and decide to keep the bad news about the casting a secret. There is no point to keep complaining and make my Mama upset; she carries such a heavy load on her frail shoulders teaching full time and taking care of our family. I picture her returning from work earlier this evening, with her hands full of heavy groceries, mostly cans and grains. Exhausted, she crashes on the kitchen chair. While, Mama amusingly describes the arguing that took place in four long lines in which she stood while getting our food stock, I stare at her wrists marked with bright red traces from the bags' straps.

"So, you had a good day at school?" Mama interrupts my thinking.

"Yes, I did." I push my worries deep inside and say, "See you in the morning, Mamochka."

She kisses my forehead and disappears into the light of the kitchen and, although I hear both of my parents just across the wall of our one-bedroom apartment, I can't help but feeling abandoned. In my bed, I turn and roll and when I finally fall asleep it's only for a short time. I wake up recalling a disturbing dream where Violeta appeared as cruel Milady[7] from "Three Musketeers" and I was Constance[8] whom she is after. My cheeks are wet from tears and I can't stop shaking. I hang my feet down from the bed and feel the warmth of Niko's coat. Curled on the floor, with my arm across his large body, I fall into a peaceful sleep at last.

---

[7] Is a spy and a murderer, and one of the dominant antagonists in *The Three Musketeers*.

[8] One of the main female characters, loyal to the Queen of France and assassinated by Milady.

Chapter 5: MAMA'S NEWS

Thick grey clouds spread across the entire sky, and although the grass is still green and the dense foliage of the state park that borders the Academy's front yard is painted in bright fall colors, my mood reflects the color of the sky. I walk to school alone, murmuring the verses of Pushkin's "Ruslan and Lyudmila" that I'm about to recite in Russian Lit class.

> On seashore far a green oak towers,
> And to it with a gold chain bound,
> A learned cat whiles away the hours
> By walking slowly round and round.
> To right he walks, and sings a ditty;
> To left he walks, and tells a tale....

I imagine a magical sea sight with wondrous mermaids and mysterious wizards from the poem. I don't feel nervous, just excited in anticipation of standing in front of my classmates and reciting the whole six verses instead of two that the teacher assigned. To me, reciting feels very much like acting, and so different from executing various *ballet pas*. My self-consciousness leaves me when I'm outside the ballet studio; with poetry there are no worries about pointing feet or stretching knees, only that special music-like rhythm of words.

When I arrive at the academy and stop by the coat room to hang my rain jacket, I meet Natasha.

"Why do we have to memorize these endless poems so often?" She questions with obvious annoyance.

I notice that her eyes look smaller than usual and the skin around them looks puffy. I figure out she stayed up late last night.

"But we were given this assignment last week and had a short day on Saturday and all Sunday to study. Did you try to learn it overnight?" Already on the stairs, we stop to curtsy to the Biology teacher; according to the Academy rules, we must curtsy to every teacher in the building.

"Yeah, I did. It somehow slipped my mind. I was looking forward to spending a weekend with my dad but he changed his plans. He ended up sending his chauffeur to take me to the movies though. I wanted you to come along and tried to call you but the phone was constantly busy."

"It was our neighbor's grandma. She talks for hours, ignoring the fact we have a joined line with that family. Papa had to bang on our ceiling with the broom stick till she finally hung up and let us use the phone."

As we enter the classroom, we greet our Russian Language and Literature teacher Alla Vladimirovna, or Allachka, as we affectionately refer to her. She meets us with her usual warm smile, looking down from the high stool on which she stands holding a watering can. Allachka returns to watering her plants on the shelves as we settle at the desk close to the black board.

During the class, the teacher calls me last to recite the poem. She approvingly nods while I deliver the six verses, and is the first one to applaud. Max yawns. When the entire class applauds, he rolls his eyes. Two of his buddies, Gena and Arthur, copy his every move. I must admit, Max's recitation was the best compared to the rest of the boys; his voice was confident and the look on his face was poised. My opponent comes from a family of actors and acting genes seem to run in his blood. Yet, he only memorized four verses. I feel victorious, but hide my joyful mood in sake of preserving Natasha's feeling; after she stumbles through her entire reciting, she spends the rest of the class hiding her face in her folded arms on top of the desk.

By the time we migrate to the neighboring classroom for our history lesson, the day grows darker and gloomier; one hardly could tell it's still morning, since outside it looks like the sun is about to set. I unhappily take the seat assigned to me by the strict history teacher, Agrippina Viktorovna. Our wooden, hard and sturdy desks are for double occupancy. Yet Agrippina insisted on me sitting alone, so no one could take an advantage of my knowledge. I feel isolated and on the spot. To make matters worse, today's subject revolves around the exile of Vladimir Lenin, the founder of the Communist party and the leader of the October Revolution. It bores me to death while Agrippina's monotonous voice makes time freeze. I cover my yawning and fight to keep my eyes open, but the soothing sound of the rain outside the window makes it really difficult. When Agrippina turns her back to me to show the slides from the projector on the white board, I use this break to briefly close my eyes. It seems only a second passes when a thunder of laugh makes me open them again. First I see Agrippina; she leans over my desk with her face so close to mine that I can distinguish the drops of sweat on her wide forehead; her breath is labored and it smells of onions and smoked fish. Horrified, I realize she has caught me asleep. And worse of all, I realize I'm clutching Agrippina's pointer in my hand, not having a clue why. Without taking her angry stare off my face, Agrippina retreats her pointer and returns to the board. The laughing dies to just a whispering and I beg for the teacher to begin speaking again. I feel frozen with the embarrassment, afraid to look up from my book and, for the first time, thankful to sit alone. The rest of the lesson I spend in some sort of trance. While Vladimir Lenin experiences the hardships of life in the remote Siberian village of Shushenskoe, all I can think of is the bell that seems to never ring.

When finally its liberating sound frees me from my exile in the world of embarrassment, my three loyal friends surround my desk and together we walk out to the hallway. Max and his friends try to catch up with us. Vera and Tanya let me and Natasha pass towards the stairs, while two girls stay behind. I hear Vera confronting Max.

"Did Mira ever do anything to you so you would take a revenge on her like that? If you didn't raise your hand and point out our friend, Agrippina would have never noticed her falling asleep."

I can't hear the rest of the conversation, since Natasha pulls me down the stairs, leaving the other two girls engaged with Max and his gang.

"It actually was kind of funny, the way you got Agrippina's pointer and swung it into her face," says Natasha already in Razdevalka.

"Why did I do that?" I finally dare to look at my friend. Her comforting voice and the laughing sparkles in her eyes help me to relax.

"I could never tell you were asleep." Sveta, who sits closest to me during history, engages in the conversation. "The whole time you supported your head with your hand and looked like the most attentive student. Until Max pointed you out to Agrippina and she realized your eyes were shut, she began poking you under your chin with her pointer; that's when you grabbed it and swung it back at her."

All the girls burst into harmonious laughter. I'm the only one not laughing, but just for a brief moment; with the next second, I join in.

In every ballet studio at the Academy *ballet barres* are attached to two walls, one wall is covered with mirrors and the one that faces outside is made of glass. My favorite *barre* is the one that is stretched parallel to the enormous window. Although during all the *barre* exercises we must look towards the center and away from the window, I always find a brief moment to glance outside at the wind in the trees and the endless sky. Now, facing the *barre*, with one leg placed on top of it, we execute various *port de bras*, bending towards and away from the leg, elongating through our limbs to improve flexibility. I feel dissolved in the beautiful "Nocturne"[9] by Chopin that Leonid plays with so much passion, when suddenly Violeta ruins my well-being.

---

[9] A short, typically piano composition of a romantic or dreamy character suggestive of night.

"I heard that you, Techenko, are the best student in class. Why don't you put more effort and energy into stretching those bumpy thighs of yours and work on your weak feet instead of notching history events and physics formulas." Violeta's voice mercilessly strikes again, ruining the beauty and purity of Chopin's sounds while turning my school accomplishments, something I always have been proud of, against me. Suddenly, I feel ashamed of my grades and of being an all "A" student. I nod, and bend toward my leg, trying to hide my face; I try not to blink while my eyes get as blurry as the windows attacked by October rain that hits the glass and rushes down its surface.

We continue with *center* work. While the first group executes *adagio*, I hide in the corner, practicing my *balance en retiré*; standing on one leg, with my other leg bent at a 90-degree angle and its pointed foot attached to the supporting leg at the knee level. I struggle to keep my supporting foot in *demi-point* position with heel high from the floor and arched instep. Soon, a painful cramp in my supporting calf forces me to give up balancing. Frustrated, I stretch it for a moment, until it is time for the second group to perform *adagio*. It begins with *développé* to the side, and when I must rise on my standing foot with other leg still lifted high in the air, I realize it happens with more ease than before and I can sustain this position longer. It's just a tiny accomplishment, yet in the long path towards perfection, such small victories over the body's limitations make ballet rewarding. Despite Violeta's comment, I leave today's class feeling satisfied.

In the evening, when the rainfall finally stops and there is even a glimpse of the stars through the remaining clouds, I accompany Mama and Niko on their walk. Outside, refreshing October air fills my lungs, also warning of an approaching chilly night. The dog happily trots ahead, while we leisurely stroll through the wide alley, hand in hand, marveling on the multicolored leaves in their fall dance; the lightest of them are pulled by the wind from the branches and whirled round and round before they finally rest on the ground. Everything around and inside of me breathes peace and contentment; even Violeta seems unimportant.

That's when Mama casually puts her arm around my shoulder and says, "Dochen'ka, today the dean of the Linguistics department called me into his office to announce my job duty will take me to Beijing. He reminded me that twice before the department assigned me to teach abroad as a part of the University's exchange program which I avoided, giving the department some valued excuses. Now I have no other choice but to accept the assignment. If I don't, my position at the university could be jeopardized."

Mama's words first reach my ears and then, like an electrical shock, strike my brain. My body stiffens and a tight knot in my throat obstructs any sound to come out from my mouth.

"How long will you be gone?" I finally manage to whisper not even wanting to hear the answer.

"Eight months."

I feel chilling cold inside. Tears begin streaming down my cheeks.

"Eight months in China! But it is thousands kilometers away from Ukraine! Without you by my side,

Violeta will completely destroy me!" I yell into the peaceful quietness of the evening.

We find ourselves standing by the lamp post; two lonely figures with a perplexed dog pacing around us. My face is buried in Mama's chest. I choke with tears and gasp for air while letting myself pour out all the humiliations I've been taking from Violeta in class within the last several weeks.

"No matter how hard I work, I only receive Violeta's brutal criticisms. Yet, she compliments Larissa, so skinny now - her skin seems transparent; Larissa often can't even finish the class, complaining of pain in her limbs. Still, this afternoon, while Lena was absent with a cold, Violeta called on Larissa to replace her in the "Jig". It's obvious Larissa can't handle this fast-paced dance, but Violeta puts her in anyway; her goal is to hurt my feelings, to break my spirit, to make me quit!"

My face is cupped in Mama's hands; she looks deep in my eyes and says, "No, she won't destroy you. Yes, it's going to be tough, but Papa and Babushka will be on your side. You have such supportive friends, too.

Ballet is your dream and Violeta can't take it away from you. Remember your first teacher Marina Ivanovna – she raised Pleiades[10] of beautiful dancers and she saw talent and promise in you. Just keep that in mind."

I hug Mama tight. She always finds wise and comforting words. I stop crying; still far from returning to my peaceful contentment with the news that burdens me now.

I pick up Niko's leash from the ground. "Let's go home" I say, taking Mama's hand. We walk in silence. There is a question that occupies my mind but I'm afraid to ask. Right before we enter the building, I finally do, "When do you leave?"

Mama's eyes meet mine; I read a painful expression in her loving stare. "I have one week to organize my absence and pack," she says hesitantly.

I squeeze Mama's hand and turn my face away from her, hiding returning tears. The day, when I wake up and start my life without my Mama is closer than I could imagine.

---

[10] A cluster of stars

Chapter 6: LOOKING FOR TROUBLE

I'm riding a bus that takes our entire class across the city from the Academy to the Ukraina Palace, Kiev's main Performing Arts Center. Just a week ago, Papa and I took a similar bus from Sheremetyevo Airport, located in the outskirts of Moscow. Suddenly, the setting on the bus evokes the memories of our farewell with Mama. I recall watching the plane taking her away to Beijing, my forehead pressed against the cold glass of the airport window. The plane soon became just a dot and then disappeared from my sight, yet I stood there much longer denying a fact that a new life, with Mama being far away and unreachable, has begun.

Recollection of those events provokes a familiar pain inside of my chest. I bite my lip to stop myself from crying. At this moment, Natasha pulls on my elbow offering an oatmeal cookie. Instantly, she catches my devastated glare. She takes my hand in hers and begins to hum my favorite song. Tanya and Vera, who sit in front of us, gaily pick up the tune. In a few minutes our bus is filled with students' singing, and the driver, who lacks radio, doesn't seem to mind.

When we arrive at the Ukraina Palace and step down from the bus, we find ourselves among numerous members of other professional and children's performing groups standing in line to enter a massive building from the rear, "Artists Entrance". Our class is about to participate in a concert dedicated to the celebration of the October Revolution. The revolution took place 69 years ago in October, yet due to a calendar change is celebrated on the seventh of November. The concert is organized exclusively for members of the Central Committee of the Communist Party and closed to regular citizens. A vast number of performers are called for such an event; everything organized for the Party must represent the massive and monumental power of the Soviet State.

"I love these events that interrupt our usual routine and allow us to miss school!" Vera drops her bag on the floor of the backstage lobby and puts her costume on top of the pile with the rest of our "Mazurka" dresses.

"If only the math teacher wouldn't give us all these extra assignments to complete at home," complains Natasha.

"I brought my math book with me. We can team up to do these assignments faster; there is always so much waiting around during these long concerts," offers Tanya.

"No kidding. Did you see all those people outside and still arriving?" Vera joins in.

"I'm surprised the Party members don't doze off in their comfy chairs surrounded by darkness during the show." I grin.

"I bet they take turns sneaking out to the banquet room. I heard about all the delicacies it offers," says Vera, patting her stomach.

"The banquet room!" Natasha and I exclaim at the same time and look at each other.

"Let's change quickly," I whisper to my friend. "We perform last before the intermission and can check out the delicacies before we dance."

I slip off my clothes and begin dressing up into the military suit. When back in September the cast list went up, I wasn't surprised Violeta gave me a boy part. Yet, casting might have nothing to do with Violeta's hatred towards me and could be caused by me being tall.

In fact, Larissa dances a boy's part too. I brush down the fabric on my pants and straighten my jacket.

"This military uniform suits your style," compliments Natasha.

"You think so, wait for the hat." I pull my head piece over my eyebrows, tucking in my long braid. "Now my manly look is complete."

"You do look like a very cute boy in your disguise." Natasha takes me under my elbow, pulling me toward the door.

"Make it back in time!" Tanya shouts at our backs.

Already in the hallway, we glance at each other and I read an excited expression in Natasha's eyes. I'm sure I have it too. My heartbeat quickens with every step in anticipation of an adventure. We rush through one hallway after another, holding hands, nervously giggling. As we pass other people, we slow down and act with confidence and awareness of where we head. When it seems we are never going to find the way that leads to the audience's half of the Palace, we finally step into the main lobby.

The banquet room is right next to it. We stick our heads in the wide opening of the double doors and gasp at the sight of long tables covered with a variety of foods I have never seen all at once in my entire twelve years life. To our biggest surprise, there is not a soul guarding this treasure. Cautiously, we step inside. The wooden panels of the floor squeak as we slowly approach the tables. I swallow and look around, nervously. The dimness of the hallway replaced by the bright light of the overhead chandelier makes me feel under the spotlight.

"What if someone catches us here?" I ask Natasha, looking back at the dark opening of the door.

"Don't worry, if we hear the footsteps, we can hide under the table. Look what a perfect hiding spot it is." I glance in a direction of where Natasha points. Snow white and hard starched, tablecloths cover all four tables, coming down all the way to the floor. Natasha's right – that could be our refuge in case someone suddenly walks in.

"Okay, let's just get a few sandwiches," I whisper to Natasha.

"Would that be wrong, I mean, would that be stealing?" Suddenly, Natasha sounds hesitant. I follow my friend's gaze and meet the stare of our country's revolutionary leader Vladimir Lenin. His oversized portrait hangs in the space between two windows, draped with heavy curtains, hiding the image from my sight when we first walked into the room. Now, the questioning expression of Lenin's grey eyes make me shiver. I sharply turn my head away from the leader and say, "I don't think so. They get all these delicacies for free. Would you say *they* work harder and deserve it more than you, or me, or our parents?" I choke on the last word, realizing that Natasha's dad is one of "they", but she seems not to notice.

Without further delay, we begin our feast.

Natasha is the first to reach for a small napkin which she uses to grab her sandwich. "This salami is out of this world! Mira, you must try it!"

"I will later. First let me taste my favorite sandwich with sprats and a slice of lemon," I say and hurry to bite into the sandwich, realizing how much I miss citrus fruits and hope to see them reappear in the stores as usual for the New Year's holidays.

"Look at the variety of cheeses!" Natasha calls from the opposite side of the room.

"I'm trying the salami; it is very yummy." I chew as fast as I can, while my eyes search for the next treat.

"Do you want a glass of Seltzer?" asks Natasha.

My mouth is so full I can only produce an agreeable "mooing" as a response. She brings me a drink and we clink our glasses.

After a few more slices of cheese, I begin to feel a slight cramping in my stomach and realize it's time to stop gobbling. Yet, my eyes just fix on several platters of sweets. I hesitate for a second, knowing I shouldn't eat any more, but I can't resist the sight of the crunchy merengue, the airy soufflé, the colorful squares of three layered jelly and my favorite marmalade candies - the lemon cloves.

Natasha and I nibble on the small bites of each dessert and drink more Seltzer.

"I feel like a balloon," complains Natasha, her hand resting on her stomach.

"That's another advantage of my loose slacks and roomy jacket." I grin, pointing out the space I still retain in my clothing. "But I feel extremely full too. It's time to head back."

As we leave, Natasha turns around and whispers, "Thanks to our Party for all the wonderful treats in here." She sighs loudly and trots after me.

We quickly cross the main lobby, still not a soul in sight, and come through the door that takes us into the long hallway, which we remember passing. What we don't remember is which way to go when the hallway splits in a fork.

"Did we take right or left here?" I suddenly feel hot and pull off my military cap.

"We took so many rights and lefts; I can't put them in order now." Natasha's big almond- shaped eyes grow even bigger; a few small wrinkles appear on her forehead. She is panicking. "What time is it? What if they are about to perform our dance?"

If anything, I'm the one who should be panicking. Violeta likes Natasha, and it's easy to imagine who will receive all the blame.

I grab Natasha's hand and pull her to the right.

"You remembered!" Natasha exclaims and I don't dispute. Yet, I can't remember anything. All I know we better move.

We run forward, holding hands while passing multiple doors on the endless wall. Suddenly a large figure steps out of the door right in front of us.

"Please, tell us how to get to the stage," begs Natasha, catching her breath.

A man gives us a suspicious look and to our horror points at the direction we just came from.

In a split second, I picture the consequences of not making it back on time and ruining the performance for the entire group.

"I wish we had never gone on our stupid adventure," I say while we sprint in the opposite direction.

"I thought you knew where to go. My bun is about to fall from all this running." I hear Natasha's sobbing and pick up my speed.

The corridor takes a smooth turn and opens into a familiar back stage lobby area, which is completely deserted.

My heart drops, but I keep rushing forward. As we come through the dark opening that leads to the stage, I almost knock our coordinator off her feet.

"Natasha! Miroslava! Where have you girls been? You missed the entire warm up."

Through the backstage wings I catch a sight of the Folkloric ensemble taking a bow and immediately sense the warmth of relief replacing the painful tension all over my body.

"We're warm alright." I grin and find my place in the already organized line of dancers. Still, there is a nervous shake in my legs: how close we were to get in the biggest trouble. My fear is interrupted by the sparkly tune of Minkus[11] music. All at once, the joy of performing for the audience sends away my nervousness and transforms me into a different world. We enter the stage, couple by couple, in a fiery "Mazurka"[12] step and

---

[11] An Austrian ballet composer and violinist.
[12] A lively dance originated in Poland.

immediately seize the audience's attention. First, all the couples create a straight line stretching all the way from the orchestra pit to the back drop. Then, boys and girls split in two separate columns, moving towards the wings. Boys execute their solo first. I feel heavy on my feet from all the food consumed and all the running. Even before the dance began, I felt my costume stuck to my skin with sweat. Now, due to the intensity of the dance and the heat from the stage lights, this unpleasant sensation has worsened. I try to focus on performing. The audience breaks into approving applause after boys complete a solo and kneel in front of the girls. I offer my sweaty hand to my partner Sveta; she takes it, and momentarily lets it go. Sveta gives me a disgusted look before leaving to perform her solo with the rest of the girls, while I manage to wipe the sweat from my palms on my pants. Next, all the boys get up from their knees, gallantly bow, and offer our hands to the girls to whirl them around the stage in a big circle.

The music grows louder and faster, our corresponding steps get quicker; and although I suffer from a growing pain in my feet and an increasing thirst, it's my favorite part of the dance and I fully indulge in the moment. As Sveta and I *pas marche* towards the corner, where the last part of the dance will begin, I suddenly hear a loud thump that breaks through the swell of the music. My first thought is that one of the stage lights went out with a burst; it has happened before. But when I turn around, I see a body in a boy's uniform, slumped on the floor. The music keeps playing but no one moves; everyone's eyes are fixed on a static figure in the middle of the stage. I can't see the dancer's face, but from the coiled black lock of hair escaping from the cap, I recognize Larissa. She's face down and looks almost dead. It seems like an eternity before someone screams in the wing and the curtain comes down. We finally move from our frozen positions and surround the body. Violeta pushes herself through the crowd and bends over the unresponsive girl. She gently rolls Larissa into her back, then kneels down and rests the girl's head on her knees. An expression of a genuine worry is on my teacher's face.

"Did someone call the doctor?" she yells while clenching Larissa's transparent wrist feeling for a pulse.

"The ambulance is on its way."

"Is there a nurse in the building?"

"She called in sick today."

"I can do CPR," a small voice proclaims from the back of the crowd.

The voice belongs to Slavik; the smallest and shyest boy in our class.

"We all learned CPR in our Military Preparedness class last week," he explains while everyone stares at him in disbelief.

Apparently Slavik took the assignment more seriously than the rest of us.

"Hurry, she's not breathing," says Violeta, pulling Slavik down next to her.

The boy kneels, crosses his small hands on top of Larissa's chest and vigorously begins to pump. I feel surprised and moved by Slavik's confidence and power. After about 30 pumps, he pulls off his cap, loudly fills up his lungs with air, pinches Larissa's nose and covers her mouth with his to give her two short breaths. Everyone gasps, witnessing the girl's chest slightly rise. Yet, she still seems breathless. When Slavik repeats the steps over again, Larissa's head moves and her eyelids open and close again.

"She is breathing!" exclaims Violeta, throwing her arms in the air.

Three people in white uniforms make their way through the crowd – a doctor and two tall male nurses carrying a stretcher. The doctor listens to the girl's breathing and motions to the nurses who hurriedly but gently lift Larissa and carries her away.

"Mira, Sveta and Lena, three of you will stay backstage. I need to cut you from the dance to keep the symmetry. Everyone else, quickly take your places!" Violeta orders with her usual impatience. When Minkus music once again fills the stage, it no longer sounds joyful to me. I sit in the darkness with my back against the wall, watching from the wings my classmates' brightly lit figures; but all I see is an empty stage with a motionless body in the middle and all I can think about is what happened to poor Larissa.

Chapter 7: FIRST SNOW

"Mira, get up already!"

Papa mercilessly turns on the overhead lamp in my room. Sudden light burns my eyes, while Papa's impatient voice hurts my feelings; Mama never woke me this way. She would sit on the edge of the bed, gently brush my messy hair off my face, then touch it softly and whisper: "It's time for my beauty to rise and shine in front of morning Aurora and the entire world."

After Papa makes sure I'm awake, he returns to the kitchen leaving me overwhelmed with self-pity; I just don't want to start another day without Mamochka by my side. I take a few steps towards the window, now fully awake by the sensation of the icy cold floor on my feet. I glance outside, expecting to see the black and grey colors of our courtyard, but am surprised by an unexpected whiteness instead. The first November snow fell overnight and is still falling. I stay by the window marveling at the large flakes that float from the sky bearing the trees under its icy blanket. Hesitantly, I finally leave the window and begin getting dressed.

After my routine breakfast of a hot oatmeal and black tea, I pull on an extra sweater and wool leggings, which fit tight on top of the long underwear. I bundle into my winter fur coat. A thick wool scarf bites and itches my neck, but according to Papa must be worn to avoid pneumonia. When I finally get outside, feeling like an Eskimo from the North Pole, the beauty of the winter scenery takes my breath away. I walk along the familiar street, yet it appears new and exciting; the trees veiled under the snow make my street look as though it shrank overnight. Later in the day, during *Classica*, when I glance out the window between our routine *barre* exercises, I decide that snow outside somehow makes everything, even our ballet studio, unusually welcoming and cozy.

In the afternoon, the snowfall increases and turns into a blizzard. This weather is odd for the beginning of November. Then, in the middle of our afternoon *Practica,* there is a loud commotion in the hallway and Violeta steps out to find the cause.

"Everybody is ordered to leave Academy," announces Violeta upon her return. "Principal Bogdanov just received a phone call about sudden disruption in the operation of the city's public transportation system."

Lena raises her hand, "Violeta Yurievna, what does 'disruption in operation' mean?"

"It means you are lucky to live in the dorm. In the weather like this with no trams or buses running, the rest of us will go home on foot." Violeta walks towards the bench collecting her sweater and purse, while all of us hold the positions she left us in when she walked out.

"And what are you all waiting for? Or you suddenly don't understand the Russian language? *Practica* is over for today. Take off your point shoes and change quickly. Calling your parents might be a good idea too, maybe they can meet you half way," adds Violeta, already at the door.

I glance at the clock – it's only five in the afternoon, not a chance that Papa is home that early. Outside, the clouds look threatening and are getting darker with every passing minute.

I catch up with Slavik on the stairs leading to Razdevalka. "Wait for Natasha and me, so we can walk together," I say to him.

I change quickly, and the three of us zoom out of the building alongside many other students heading home. I hear someone calling Natasha's name and spot a skinny man in the suit standing next to the open door of the shiny black "Volga"[13]. It's Natasha's dad.

"Can you can get home by subway?" he asks as we approach the automobile.

Slavik and I shake our heads. "No, we can't. Bye Natasha, see you tomorrow," I try to sound cool and indifferent yet wish Natasha's dad would not show up. Or Larissa, who lived in my direction, was still at the Academy. We get on our way and Slavik keeps quite while I try to recall how many days have passed since

---

[13] A car brand named after the longest river in Europe, also regarded as the national river of Russia.

Violeta's announcement in class about Larissa dropping out of the Academy.

The easiest way to walk in this snow is by following the tram's tracks. Since its operations got suspended just a few hours ago, the pathway is still clear compared to the sidewalks. The snow comes down hard and sticks to our faces, blinding our eyes. There is no beautiful scenery as I witnessed this morning; in fact, there is no scenery at all. We are surrounded with an endless whiteness. We walk in silence. I feel tired with my heavy fur coat pulling down on my shoulders and, although Slavik trudges right beside me, I feel very lonely.

When I approach the turn to my street, I find Papa standing at the corner of the intersection. "I'm so happy to see you." I manage to whisper through my frozen lips, squeezed by Papa's bear hug. I conceal my icy face in his puffy jacket and already feel warmer.

When we get home, Papa takes restless Niko for a walk, while I put a kettle on the stove and turn on another burner to warm my hands. It's cold in the apartment. I touch the metal radiator under the window in the kitchen and don't feel enough heat coming from its surface.

While we sit down at the kitchen table to eat our simple dinner of barley soup, Papa turns on the radio. We listen to the voices delivering news from several places around Central Ukraine. They report on catastrophic situations unfolding in small towns blocked by the snow, and about the complete shutdown of the capital's transportation system.

"They blame it on the snow, yet this blizzard wasn't disastrous. The quality and condition of the plowing machinery in our country, that's what is disastrous. It's old and outdated, yet all the money is put into competing with America over who has more rockets." Papa rubs the top of his wide forehead furrowed by deep wrinkles. I realize it's not just the snow storm that troubles Papa.

"Papa, what do they need these rockets for?"

"To keep us safe, according to the government; if we are equal or better equipped with nuclear weapons than the Americans, it will make them afraid of us and keep a peaceful balance between two of the most powerful empires."

I feel sleepy and confused by Papa talking politics. Yet, I do catch two words which I understand well.

"How can nuclear weapons keep the peace? We had a nuclear plant accident in Chernobyl, and many people died or got hurt. What if…"

"Let's get you to bed now," Papa cuts me off, "and don't worry, there is going to be no "what ifs". Gorbachev[14] seems like a smart guy, the youngest among all the General Secretaries of the Communist Party. He is open to communication with the American president. The whole world watched in horror at what happened in Chernobyl, and no one will let…" I hear Papa's voice getting more distant as I drift into sleep.

"Mira, open your eyes, you need to change for bed."

---

[14] A final leader of the Communist Party of the Soviet Union from 1985 until 1991.

"Papochka[15], can I keep my clothes on? I'm so cozy," I murmur, imagining how unpleasantly cold my pajamas would feel.

Papa sighs but doesn't argue. He lifts me, bundled in a wool blanket like a thick blinetz[16], and carries me to my bed. As soon as Papa leaves my room Niko jumps up. And even though I feel crowded with dog's large body occupying half of my bed space, I let him stay to keep me warm on this cold November night.

---

[15] An affectionate word for Papa.

[16] A thin, crepe-like pancake with filling.

Chapter 8: FIGHT

We survive the next two days in a cold city paralyzed by the merciless snow storm. Many students and teachers are forced to commute to school on foot. Finally, it's Saturday, which means a shorter day at the Academy. Waiting for the tram that finally resumed operations, I try to keep warm, jumping from one foot to the other and blowing into my mittens for the warm air to bounce into my frozen face. The tram approaches, but I realize there is no chance I can get on. It's packed so tight that people's coats stick out between tram's folded doors. I throw my bag's strap across my chest and start walking instead.

Miraculously, midway another tram catches up with me, but I'm already hopelessly late for the Military Preparedness class. When I get to school, I consider skipping the class, but change my mind after hanging up my coat, and fly up two staircases to the classroom. The teacher, Vladimir Fedorovich Klimenko or Fedor, meets me with an icy look and keeps me standing in the door's threshold while he scolds me that every missed minute of his class can cost me a life in case the enemy attacks and I don't know how to properly put on a gas mask. I hold his stare yet barely listen to his lecturing; instead I try to focus on something positive, like spending tonight at Babushka's.

"I'm sorry to be late. The tram was full. I had to walk half way to school." I try to defend myself, knowing in advance it is pointless to ask for understanding from Fedor; a middle-aged Lieutenant-in-reserve who never cares about anything except his drills.

"Well, Techenko, for two days we had a large snow fall. Did you expect that while you were whirling around in your dance class or dozing in your warm bed, some good citizens plowed the snow from the tracks, so you could commute to school like a queen?" Fedor pauses to make sure everyone gets his point.

"Plan for disastrous conditions and defy them - that's what every conscious Soviet citizen must do," he pauses again and scans my classmates' faces with his suspicious eyes hidden under huge bushy eyebrows. "You never can be too ready, and you always must be on a lookout. Now, Techenko, take a seat and copy from the board the order of steps for disassembling and cleaning the rifle."

I sit on the hard seat, which is attached to the old fashion school desk, and hurriedly open my notebook. Fedor comes by, stands behind my shoulder and says, "When the bell rings, don't rush out the class; you'll have to stay and watch me demonstrate the rifle dissembling that you missed."

I stand up, salute and reply, "Yes, Tovarisch[17] Klimenko!"

The rest of the short day goes by fast and much smoother. There is no *Practica* on Saturdays, so at three o'clock in the afternoon when the last bell of the day releases us from biology, I rush downstairs to Razdevalka. I quickly pack my ballet uniform to be washed and point shoes to be mended over the weekend.

"My dad is coming to pick me up," says Natasha as she stacks her sky blue robe into her school bag. She seems to avoid looking at me. I realize she must feel uncomfortable not having to walk home or take a crowded tram like everyone else.

---

[17] Is a Russian word for a comrade in arms.

"I'm actually heading to Babushka's," I answer.

"Oh, then we can give you a ride to the subway station!" exclaims Natasha.

Maybe because it's Saturday or due to another, unknown-to-me reason, Natasha's dad instructs his driver to take me all the way to where my Babushka lives, which is two stops on the tram, three stops on the subway, and another three on the bus or the trolleybus. By car it takes only twenty minutes to arrive at Babushka's apartment building, climb four stories of the narrow staircase and ring the bell of her apartment.

"How in the earth did you get here so fast?" Babushka hugs me tight but then, instead of letting me into the living room, gently pushes me back into the hall outside of the door.

"I was on my way to Gastronom[18], the neighbor told me they expect an afternoon sugar delivery; and if we are lucky, we might even get some butter," she says.

I notice that Babushka already has her coat on. She looks in the mirror and fixes her pretty mink hat, the one she made herself, along with many other hats and

---

[18] A food market.

clothing that everyone in the family wears. Babushka hands me a sack knitted of multiple threads, which serves for every household as an indispensable grocery carrier, strong and roomy.

We walk about two blocks towards the square where a big grocery store is; yet before we even see its doors we spot a long line that spirals outside.

“Mira, do you have enough clothes underneath your coat?” Babushka always worries about me being underdressed. “Do you have a double layer on your legs? How about your hands?”

I try to convince her that I’m fine, but soon realize that prolonged standing in the minus fifteen degrees air is much tougher than walking in the same temperature.

Over an hour passes, and we begin having doubts about the sugar delivery. It might have been just a rumor that quickly passed from neighbor to neighbor, gathering such a large crowd. Babushka tries to persuade me to return to the apartment.

“I will not leave you. Let’s just go home together and fry the rye toasts on the sunflower oil,” I resist.

"Not after we've waited this long. Look, there is a commotion by the door. I think people are finally getting into the store."

But Babushka is wrong, people scatter into different directions and we hear someone's terrifying scream, "Please, stop, you are hurting him!"

My heartbeat stalls when I see two men punching and kicking each other. When one of them turns to face us, I block my eyes with my hands from the image of blood covering the man's face. Babushka shields me inside her shawl. I hear multiple voices from the crowd demanding the men to quit and for someone to call the police and an ambulance. I push the fabric away and dare to peek: a man with a bloody face lays on the ground and a woman crying hysterically hunches over him. The "victor" is held back by two random men who bravely stepped out of the crowd to stop the fight.

"Let's go, Mirochka. I just remembered the plum jam I've stored this summer. It'll be a delicious spread on toast." Babushka realizes that I'm still in shock from what we've just witnessed; she grabs me under my elbow and pulls my frozen stature away from the scene.

By the time we are back at the apartment, it is dark outside and Babushka's tiny kitchen feels especially warm and cozy. A square dining table occupies most of the space. There is also a stove, a sink, a small countertop between them and a corner couch with soft leatherette upholstery. With two more low stools, there is barely any space left for people, so the fridge is placed in the niche in the small hall by the entrance door.

I sit on my knees on the comfy couch, with my feet bent under, while Babushka passes me a cutting board with a half loaf of rye bread. I slice the bread while she pours sunflower oil in the hot pan. A pleasant scent immediately rises above it and drifts towards me. Babushka is the first one to break the silence we kept on a back walk to the apartment.

"Have you received a letter from Mama yet?" She asks placing the first portion of sliced bread on the pan.

"No, but I really hope it'll arrive next week. I mailed three letters to her already. I miss talking to her so much. When I write, it feels a little bit like talking and I imagine her listening. Then I picture how she would react. Sometime it's very helpful, other times I end up in tears wishing to hear her real voice."

Babushka places a bowl of hot vermicelli soup in front of me and gently strokes my head. I look up at her and without any words I know she misses Mama a lot, too, and worries about her even more.

"My goodness, I almost burned our last slices of bread!" Babushka throws her arms in the air and hurries to the stove. Luckily, she only needs to take two steps to get there. She flips the toasts and then pours boiling water into the fat porcelain teapot embellished with green apples and red strawberries.

"Let's have tea and watch some television. Take this table cloth and cover the table in the living room, please."

After the steaming tea cups and delicious smelling toasts spread with jam are served on top of the small round table, I turn on the TV.

"Oh my God, I almost forgot about Gorbachev's 'After the Summit' summary speech!" Babushka doesn't really believe in God, nor does she believe in politics and its positive influence on the Soviet people. Yet, she often mentions the Creator and never misses political events.

Babushka's old black and white TV finally warms up and the image of a man with a wide forehead and a noticeable birth mark in the shape of an island appears on the screen. Gorbachev talks about food shortages, caused by many of our country's resources being put into the 'Space Race'. I enjoy chewing my crusty toast, while half-listening about the ongoing competition between the Soviet Union and the evil United States in building and testing nuclear rockets. Before Gorbachev's appointment, the news reported that we were ahead of the entire planet in everything. These open discussions about problems and shortages is what our new leader of the Communist Party calls *Glasnost.*

"Let's see what all these reformations called *Perestroika,* that Gorbachev is eager to implement, will do for us," comments Babushka. "It's sad your grandfather didn't live to see this day when we can finally speak up without hiding behind closed kitchen doors."

I nod and ask Babushka to change the channel at last. I flip twice through all four programs and select a movie made in the fifties or maybe sixties. I can't really tell the difference. There is a lot of singing and dancing in this movie; everyone seems happy and careless. I know from my grandparents' memories that postwar time was harsh and difficult. I think about our present with long lines and the scarcity of basic groceries like sugar and butter. People lose patience and some turn into beasts like the men fighting today. For a split second I think of Gorbachev and wish he could make our lives safer and more prosperous, and then I return into the black and white screen, immersed in the singing and dancing of its happy inhabitants.

Chapter 9: REFUGIES

In my world of Ballet, politics and reformations attract very little attention, compared to the freezing conditions in the Academy's building. Five days of zero temperatures, even during the day, have forced us to wear our coats and hats inside the classrooms. Though for dance classes we wear our usual attire, adding some thick long underwear and sweaters over the tights and leotards. Dancing in such freezing conditions is a total torture; our toes never manage to get warm, our noses are bright red and we breathe white puffs of steam.

Finally, the Academy director makes a decision to shorten all the Dance curriculum classes by half.

"The performance is coming up and I still haven't chosen the pair of point shoes I'm going to dance in," complains Natasha looking like a pitiful bird sitting on top of the radiator in our Razdevalka.

I place my hands on top of its metal surface and barely feel any warmth.

"They said on the radio that the temperature is expected to rise at the end of this week. It's not like we live in the North Pole; it should get warmer soon." I try to cheer my friends.

Vera and Sveta come inside carrying steaming glasses with yellowish liquid. It tastes more like sweetened water than tea, but it is hot and feels good to drink as well as to hold in our cold hands. We take turns going back to cafeteria to fetch more tea.

"Girls, Violeta Yurievna is waiting for you. Did you forget you have *Practica* at four?" our home classroom teacher calls from the hallway.

We put thick socks over our ballet slippers, and instead of our usual robes, we keep our coats on until we get to the ballet studio gallery. There, we pile them on the bench by the studio door and each curtsy before taking our places at the *barre*.

"Make a circle and start running to warm up," Violeta orders.

We run several laps and I hear everyone's labored breathing; I feel cramps in my gut, yet my feet are still numb.

When Violeta finally allows us to stop, we gather our point shoes from the radiator where we placed them to get warm; they are still freezing cold and stiff. Sitting on the floor, we repeatedly blow inside of the shoes and hurry to put them on. Violeta demands we take our sweaters off so she can clearly see our backs and arms. Shivering, we obey her order, then, begin the practice.

Right in the middle of the Shostakovich's Waltz, which we rehears to perform this coming weekend at the semiannual Academy's performance, a boy from our grade suddenly opens the door and shouts, "Quick, save your stuff, there is a flood in the basement!"

We turn our eyes to Violeta and see her nodding and pointing towards the door. I run in front of our group, thinking of my almost new boots. By the time we get down to the basement, the hallway is already covered with a thin layer of water that smells like a sewer. We can't walk through in our precious point shoes, so we take them off. With only thin tights over my feet, I cautiously step into the water and immediately feel its coldness. My nose is also repulses by the awful smell. As I continue through the hallway towards the door to our Razdevalka, I hear the Academy's handyman yell, "It's the pipes in the boys' showers, they gave in!"

I burst into Razdevalka, all the girls right behind me, and everyone shouts at the same time, "Oh no, our stuff!"

It's not only boys' showers, our pipes ruptured too, and a powerful flow of water surges in. Multiple objects are floating everywhere. We pull out our boots from the water, grab our bags from the lockers, and walk back to the dry safety of the stairs. The dance teachers gather at the first floor's foyer; they pity us and send us to the bathroom to clean our feet, but the water in the bathroom is shut off. Natasha suggests we go up to the Russian Lit classroom since Allachka usually stays late.

Our teeth chatter uncontrollably as we pull off the wet tights, standing on the freezing floor of the Russian classroom. Alla Vladimirovna turns on her kettle. Tanya gets her robe from the bag and wipes her feet; everyone follows her example and then quickly gets dressed.

"And now what?" asks Vera, pointing towards the row of sad looking boots standing in a puddle of water. "What do we wear to go home?"

"Let me go to the teacher's lounge and make some phone calls," says Allachka as she pours boiling water into a tea pot. "Maybe your parents can bring you a spare pair of shoes."

"I have a pair of rain boots that someone can borrow," says Vita, "We all need to get to the dorm and find more footwear for the city girls to borrow."

"That's an excellent idea, Vita!" exclaims Allachka, "Now, the question is, how do you all get to the dorm?"

"It just one block away, we wrap our feet in plastic bags and put our boots on."

"That wouldn't work. First, where do we find enough plastic bags? Plus, we can't afford your dry feet getting wet again, and in those boots they inevitably will."

"Here, gather around this space heater, you mustn't get sick when a big performance is around the corner."

Allachka disappears for a minute into her small storage room and comes back with three cups. "You'll have to share these." She leaves again and brings a cardboard box full of white squares. "Here is the sugar." She serves the auburn colored tea and leaves us to enjoy it.

While we sip the aromatic fluid and finally feel our frozen toes thaw, Allachka makes a trip to the dorm and returns with five pairs of rubber boots. Lena, Vita and three other girls walk back first. By the time Tanya and I wash the cups, Allachka brings back the boots and, finally, the city girls leave the Academy.

When, later that evening, I hurry through the door of our apartment, I can barely wait to tell Papa about the flooded basement and the challenge of getting back home.

"All's well that ends well," says Papa, "I sure hope your boots are not damaged." He pulls out a thick stack of old newspapers. "Here, stuff these inside and put them next to the oven."

"The whole Academy building will smell terribly tomorrow." Papa shakes his head.

"But we don't go to school tomorrow!" I exclaim. "For the rest of the week, we have rehearsals at the Theater."

"You are lucky then. Please, help me with dishes, since I assume you don't have any homework for tomorrow and I must finish an upcoming project."

"Sure Papochka." I carry our two plates to the sink and wash them with the rest of the dishes, listening to the monotonous clucking of the typewriter and the loud snoring of Niko who is stretched on the floor next to the open oven.

In the morning, Papa and I walk together to the subway station. After descending a long stretch of escalator, we wait for the train to arrive. There is a slight warm breeze coming from the air vents that smells of train tracks and underground humidity. The train arrives and we squeeze ourselves into one of its packed carts.

"Good luck for your rehearsal today," whispers Papa into my ear.

"I have no worries about it," I whisper back, "all I dance is a Waltz and it's in a large group. Also, a couple of days ago, during the run through of the entire performance, the Head of the Ballet department commented on my artistry, and since then Violeta hasn't been picking on me."

"Oh, good," sighs Papa and kisses my forehead; the doors slide open and I step out on the platform of my station. I wave as the train takes Papa away and walk towards the escalator that will take me up to the surface. Outside, my ascending continues along the steep street. By the time the gorgeous building of the Kiev Opera House appears in front of me, I feel I've completed my ballet warm-up. I enter the Theater from its back door, the entrance used by many world renowned dancers for the last hundred years. As I reach white marble stairs, Natasha catches up with me and we ascend to the second floor together. We travel through a skinny hallway, passing multiple doors, make-up rooms for the corps de ballet, and finally find a door that has a paper with our dance's name written on it. Inside, we settle our bags on top of the loveseat and each sit in front of the armoire. In the room, white drapes hide a small window that looks out the wintery street. The loveseat and chairs are made of red velvet; there is also a matching red rug on the wooden floor. The dressing room is a whole different world compared to the Academy, warm and luxurious, making us feel like refugees. Suddenly, Violeta bursts into the room and blows away our sense of tranquility and happiness.

"Since you are only going to mark through the dances today, we won't have a complete class before the rehearsal."

"Yes, Violeta Yurievna." Natasha and I nod in unison. Even despotic Violeta seems nicer in this warm and welcoming environment. The rest of the girls arrive, greet Violeta, and remain as statues, still and silent. When the silence becomes uncomfortable, there is a knock and the orchestra's young conductor sticks his head between the threshold and a slightly opened door.

"Good morning, Violeta Yurievna, do you have a minute to go through the scores of the Waltz with me; I need to make sure I'm aware of all the cuts."

"Of course, Vitaliy Sergeevich." Violeta praises the man with her rare smile. She gets up and bends over to catch her purse. In that moment the conductor winks at us. I'm so grateful, I feel like hugging the man.

Peacefully chattering, we change into our ballet attire.

"No coats needed," says Vera, slipping into her robe.

"Who wants to take a stroll to the cafeteria?" asks Tanya, "I brought some money remembering all the goodies they usually sell there."

"I didn't think of that," sighs Natasha.

"We'll buy for you," says Vita.

"Yes, let all the dorm girls treat the city girls today!" exclaims Lena and the rest of the girls make an approving sound.

As we finish our satisfying snacks of salami sandwiches and foamy sodas, we hear the music of the first number coming from the speaker. Our dance is fifth in the program but there are no doubts that Violeta is already looking for us, so we rush towards the stage.

On our way, we pass a few members of the Opera House's ballet troupe and curtsy to them. We hear loud singing in German before we turn the corner and meet a heavy built member of the opera troupe who bows to us with unexpected grace. The costume lady pushes a rack with luxuriously embellished gowns; for tonight's opera, I guess. The Opera House building is five stories high; the space occupied by the stage and everything around it belongs to the artists and everyone who helps the magic on stage come to life. The Opera members possess multiple practice rooms on the third floor and a large auditorium for orchestra rehearsals. The Ballet troupe members have three spacious studious, one of which is the size of a stage. The set and costume designers and artists retain the space on the last floor of the building, on top of the stage and under the roof.

We drop our robes by the stage wings and begin rehearsal. I love the feeling of being on stage, even if we only shift from one formation to the other, giving the light designer an opportunity to choose the right color and shade for our dance. It gives me a chance to stare into the lit auditorium, now empty but always stunning. Multiple rows of red velvet chairs spread across the ground floor. Many small boxes are attached to the wall and to each other following the semi-circled shape of the theater, resembling a bee hive turned inside out. The crown molding on the boxes' outer walls and their rails are painted cream with additions of gold. The beige and gold field flowers embrace an enormous chandelier in the center of the theater's high ceiling. Hundreds of miniature interconnected crystals dang from its base in the shape of sparkling waterfalls. Even when the lights are dim, the theater's royal beauty takes my breath away. It also makes me feel elite; to dance on this stage and be a part of this world makes all the sweat and blood we leave in the ballet studio worth of our chosen profession.

Chapter 10: SAVING THE DAY

On the day of the show, Violeta changes the call time for our class from five to three in the afternoon. Having us at the theater four hours before the performance gives her an opportunity to torment us with full length class and an array of negative comments and emotions.

There are no scheduled ballet or opera performances for two days as the theater is given to the Academy's students. The Ballet troupe members are off this afternoon, which offers us the luxury of taking class in the theater's largest studio. Flat on my back, while executing *floor barre*, I try to stay focused while staring at the surroundings. The walls of the theater studio are painted in pale blue; the high windows with arched tops are draped with white sheer curtains. There is also molding on the high ceiling and a small replica of the crystal chandelier that resembles the one in the theater.

As we begin our *pliés* on the *barre*, I'm surprised not to see Natasha, and wonder if her dad called Violeta with some sort of excuse which only works for kids from families with government connections. During the first few exercises, my body feels stiff and unresponsive. But as we get to *rond de jambe par terre*, the fourth movement in Vaganova's[19] structured order of ballet class technique, and execute a stretch with various bending of the body and a balance at the end, I gain control over my body. I hold my leg in a curved position of *attitude derrière,* enjoying a long balance on highly arched supporting foot.

When we continue our class in the center, the large space of the studio gives my movement limitless quality; the satisfactory feeling of freedom and enjoyment of stirring the air with my arms fulfill my body and soul. The studio's mirrors are beautiful and true to the image they reflect, compared to the ones in the Academy. I might still be the one with the heaviest thighs and imperfect feet, but I suddenly see myself as a dancer: elongating through my limbs in the long *balances* of *adagio* or soaring through the air in the high leaps.

---

[19] A Russian ballet training system founded by Agrippina Vaganova, that fused elements of the French romantic style with the virtuosity of the Italian technique.

I feel sorry when class ends, which hasn't happened since Violeta became my teacher. I wish this very instant I could talk to Mama and share with her the way I felt in class. As I daydream while walking toward our changing room, Violeta almost knocks me off my feet.

"Natasha is running a high fever. There is no way she will be able to perform tonight." Violeta's face is red and she gasps for air as she speaks. "Techenko, you are her understudy, but will you fit in her costume?"

Even during an emergency, when Violeta knows I'm the one who can save the day, she finds a way to hurt my feelings.

An hour later, after we briefly run the "Jig" with me taking Natasha's spot, I still tremble as I attempt to apply make-up.

"The Opera House is a magical place." I turn around on my chair and glance at the rest of my classmates. "Only an hour ago I was as calm as a cow in the pasture and look at me now, this is the third time I've tried to make my eyes look even and failed." Girls laugh and Vita volunteers to help me with an eye liner.

I stand in front of the mirror dressed in Natasha's Jig costume, which only had to be lengthened at the bottom of the skirt. I feel anxious, realizing a challenge of not being prepared enough to perform; cast as an understudy, I didn't run the Jig during the last two weeks due to our shortened practices. "Did Violeta purposefully set me up in order to witness my failure on this famous stage?" I question myself and wish Mama could be in the audience tonight.

Violeta comes by the room to check on our readiness. She is surprised to see how well the costume fits, but then her eyes fix on my face. I freeze expecting a painful verdict.

"Who did your hair?" She demands.

"The small lady with short grey hair," I reply.

Violeta disappears behind the door, leaving me question what is wrong with my hair. Vera approaches and squeezes my hand. Looking straight into my eyes she says in the most comforting voice, "Don't worry, it might be the flower arrangement she didn't like, or the way the hair dresser laid the ribbon."

I nod but expect the worst, and here it comes. Violeta returns with small lady obediently shuffling behind her.

"Sit," commands Violeta, and I immediately obey.

"Her ears stick out too much, they must be glued like this," she presses both of my ears tightly to my head.

The small lady places a bottle with yellow substance on the table in front of me. The label reads: "Theatrical glue for beards and mustaches". Then, the lady produces a strip of white fabric from the pocket of her apron and measures the circumference of my head. Violeta steps back and lets the lady apply a thick layer of glue behind each of my ears. While Violeta holds my ears pressed against my head, the lady wraps the fabric band around my head to hold my ears in place.

"Keep it on for ten minutes, dear, so the glue will dry," the small lady's voice is soft as her hands but all I feel is the coldness of humiliation. When I dare to look in the mirror, I see a pathetic looking girl with a ridiculous white band around her head.

"That will work, thank you, Vladimirovna," says Violeta with satisfaction.

Right at this moment, we hear a loud crackling from the radio followed by an announcement: "The show will begin in fifteen minutes".

Violeta herds us towards the stage. The hallway is filled with students and occasional teachers. I feel everyone's stare. When I almost reach a safety of the door to the stage, I hear a loud voice firing at my back.

"What happened to you, Techenko, have you suffered a head injury? And still going to perform, that's the spirit!" It's Max and his gang. I hear their merciless giggling as I escape into the darkness of the backstage.

The space behind the back drop of the stage is as big as the stage itself. Sometime it's crowded with monumental sets used during Operas like "Aida" or for Ballets like "Le Corsair". But it's free from the sets now, which gives me an opportunity to run the dance once again. Three girls from the "Jig" help with last minute comments.

"Who is my partner?" I ask, after Sveta tells me to make sure I'm aligned with my partner after our entrance.

"It's Max," she mumbles the answer.

Can this day get any worse? I pull off the band that holds my ears and the ribbon falls from my hair. The orchestra hits the chords of the first dance while I rush out through the door and back to the hallway to find the closest mirror and fix my head piece. A pretty girl with scared eyes stares back at me. I pick up my dress's puffy skirt and strike a first pose of the dance, at the same time forcing a smile. I like how it looks and carry this image all the way back to the stage.

"Ready?" whispers Lena in the darkness of the stage's wing.

"Yes, I'm ready." I whisper back, feeling excitement and anticipation rushing through my blood.

Chapter 11: EXPULSION

One week has passed since our performance at the Theater. The day we returned to the Academy, I felt famous for having "saved the day" as the director of the Academy described my performing the "Jig". It boosted my confidence to a point that Violeta's repetitive attacks in class left me unfazed. Until today, when I feel vulnerable and sheep-like scared again, waiting to find out my first semester grade for *Classica.*

While our homeroom teacher passes around the grade journals, my whole body begins to tremble. When I get mine, I put it on top of the desk and stare at its cover. Finally, I force my shaking hands to search for the current page. When I see a brutal "C" thickly written in red and staring at me from the corner of a page, I quickly slam closed my journal. Yet, there are some words written under the grade I must read. So I browse through the pages again and read a short note stating: "Due to a critical situation, a meeting with a parent is requested."

Suddenly, I feel a lack of oxygen and ask the teacher to be excused. Once in the fourth floor girls' room, I let myself cry. My hopes for a better grade after a successful performance at the Theater are crushed again by Violeta's high heels. Sitting on the floor with my back next to the radiator, I find comfort in hugging my knees, my head resting on top. I rock back and force, and sob until there are no more tears to cry. I wonder how long I have stayed here and if everyone has gone to *Practica* already. Natasha must have looked everywhere for me. Not caring about the consequences of missing today's *Practica*, I walk the hallway and stick my head into the Russian Lit classroom. After receiving Allachka's approving nod, I step inside.

"How much are you missing on the script?" asks the teacher, peering at me through her oversized reading glasses.

At once I realize she can tell I was crying, yet I try to focus on her question.

"I have most of it done. Do you have a minute to look it over?"

I pull out a thick notebook from my bag and bring it to the teacher's desk. On the cover, in big letters is written "The Snow Queen". Back in November, while all our dance practices where cut in half due to the freezing conditions, we spent our long afternoons in the Russian classroom. During one such afternoon, the idea of putting together a play sparked among us.

While the teacher is occupied with the script, I scribble a series of pointless monograms and ornaments on a piece of paper. My thoughts roam around the play, then switch to ballet, Mama, and somehow end with what we'll have for dinner tonight.

"Mira," Allachka takes off her glasses and looks straight into my eyes, "this is well-written. I haven't finished reading, but I already see that with some minor changes your script is going to work. You have quite a talent."

"Thank you, Alla Vladimirovna." The teacher's words sound like a music to my ears, but I can't help wondering if it's her kind nature and desire to erase my sadness that make her complement me. Even though I knew the Brothers' Grimm fairy tale well, it was a very difficult task to convert the story into a play, a script with only dialog and brief descriptions of scenery.

"Alla Vladimirovna, could you also help me with assigning the roles?"

"Certainly. How long can you stay this afternoon?"

"As long as you can keep me here," I answer and really mean it. I have no intention to show up for *Practica* today, and no desire to go home to an empty apartment; Papa has a late meeting tonight.

I hardly realize how much time has passed when Natasha finally finds me. I wave the note book at her, proudly showing her a complete script.

"Cool!" exclaims Natasha. "When do we start rehearsals? How about the parts? Can you tell me who am I going to be in the play?"

Allachka and I exchange the looks.

"Let us plan to meet tomorrow. Around this same time, we will gather everyone and announce the parts," says Allachka. "In the meantime, I will type the script for each character, so everyone can take it home tomorrow and begin memorizing their parts."

I pack my bag while Natasha stands beside me. I read a questioning expression in her big grey eyes.

Before I give the notebook back to the teacher, I briefly open it to the page with the characters and the names of the students next to them. Natasha fixes her gaze on the page. When she turns away from it, her lips are touched with a satisfying smile.

All the way home we talk about the play. Not a word is said about Violeta, the grades, or the skipped *Practica*. But no matter how excited I feel about the play and my role in putting it together, deep inside my worry about Papa's meeting with Violeta grows bigger and bigger.

The next day, I barely can wait until all the classes are over; I'm full of nervous excitement about presenting the script and the cast list to my classmates. *Practica* flies by fast; since Violeta seems to be coming down with a cold, she lets us run our *variations* without many corrections.

Finally, everyone is gathered in the Russian Lit classroom. I read out loud parts of the script and then the cast list. I try to sound confident, but my trembling voice deceives me. When I finish, Max immediately raises his hand.

"How come you chose yourself to play the role of the Queen?"

I freeze in silence and the question hangs in the air until Allachka comes to my rescue, "Since Larissa left the Academy, Mira is the tallest girl in your class and has the right stature to play the Queen. Besides, she has an excellent memory to recite multiple lines as well as great stage presence."

I feel embarrassed the teacher stepped in for my protection. Max rolls his eyes. Allachka catches it and continues.

"The only person who equals Mira's acting skills is you, Max. Would you consider playing the Snow Queen yourself?"

The classroom fills with loud laughter. I look at Max and catch a shade of embarrassment sliding over his face. I can't deny that satisfaction is mine now.

Roaming around the classroom, I hand out the script pages. Then I notice the time on the clock above Allachka's desk. It's past six o'clock. Papa was supposed to meet with Violeta at six. My joyful mood quickly changes to panic. What will she tell him? Will she insist on me losing a few kilos? Or complain that I don't stretch my knees enough and that my feet must work sharper and quicker?

I tell Allachka about the meeting and hesitantly leave the classroom filled with loud chatting and laughing. They all are so lucky to be talking about the scenery and costumes while I must face Papa and the consequences of the meeting.

I shuffle my feet to Razdevalka, pack my bag and drag it back to the second floor. I stop one door before the entrance to the teachers' lounge, drop my bag on the floor and rest my back against the wall. I try to think about the play, recall the amusing scene with Max, and for a brief moment succeed in taking my thoughts away from what's happening behind that door. Then, the door squeaks in its hinges and opens. Papa slightly bends forward to get through; Violeta follows. They seem not to notice me and I freeze, regretting I can't walk through the wall. Papa shakes Violeta's hand, thanking her for her time and explanations. When

Violeta returns to the lounge and the door loudly closes behind her, I finally begin breathing again.

Papa turns around, meets my questioning gaze and walks towards me.

"Hi, daughter." He forces a smile.

"What did she say?" I grab Papa's elbow and try to stop him, yet he keeps walking towards the stairs.

"Let's get outside."

"No, tell me! Tell me now!" I want to scream. Then I realize that in the silence of the empty but not completely deserted Academy, everyone will hear my plea. I clench my teeth and follow Papa towards the exit.

We go outside and walk through the alley, along the Academy's building, next to the gallery of the ballet studios that are revealed to the outsider's eye through the glass walls. The lights in the last two studios are still on. The windows look like humongous TV screens with dancing figures. I recognize the Academy's seniors and wonder how it would feel to be about to graduate and join a professional troupe. I try to picture myself five long years later, getting ready for the final Government exams attended by directors of the Ballet troupes from the major Ukrainian cities. Based on their judgments, likes and dislikes, job offers are given. I imagine rehearsing for the very last appearance in the student annual performance at the Opera House. Could I earn the privilege of performing an entire *pas de deux?*[20] Such a privilege is only given to a few graduating students each year.

"What an unpleasant woman!" exclaims Papa, interrupting my thoughts. "I'm not going to repeat everything she said about your feet and your knees – you must have heard that a thousand times already; her main demand was for you to slim down before your Classica exam in May." Papa pauses, and because I don't hear anything new or threatening in his words, I immediately feel all my muscles relax.

Unexpectedly, Papa continues, "The way Violeta worded her conditions was the following – your daughter's shape is unacceptable for the Academy's standards. Unless it changes within the next four

---

[20] A dance duet in which two dancers, typically a male and a female, perform ballet steps together.

months, I must consider suspending her from the Academy at the end of this school year."

I don't say a word and my feet never stop moving. When we reach a tram station, I turn in the direction of home and keep walking. Papa follows. Air traps in my lungs and when I finally try to speak, all that comes out is a coarse sobbing. Suddenly there are no feelings or thoughts left, I feel hollow inside and the only sensation I'm aware of is the crispness of the December air that cools the burning heat from the tears streaming down my cheeks.

Niko waits for us by the door and jumps on me as soon as Papa opens it. I push the dog away, annoyed by his careless joyfulness. Immediately regretting it, I bend over and embrace his strong neck. I pull him closer to me and find a comfort in burying my face in his thick mane. Not feeling a drop of hunger, I retreat to my room. There, I hunch over my desk, find a piece of paper and write, "My dearest Mamochka," I begin my letter, "I truly hate to tell you this, but after today it doesn't make sense to keep you unaware of the way Violeta has been treating me all this time." I continue my letter by listing every episode that occurred since Mama left; I describe in details Violeta's sarcasm regarding my school grades, the glued ears and her final threat during today's meeting. I put down my pen and gaze outside: my beloved poplars behind the window are lit by the full moon. The trees look so calm, the gorgeous moon so careless. I picture myself as just a speck in the endless universe and suddenly my problems seem small and unimportant. Staring at the moon, I crumble the letter and push it inside the desk's drawer. I reach for the overhead shelf, crammed with two rows of books, and pull out the one with dancers in red unitards on its cover. I often refer to this photo book seeking inspiration from the images of ballet legends. Turning the pages, I peer at the famous Soviet ballerinas and ballet dancers. I'm familiar with their beginnings and aware of how many of them had to battle their physical imperfections and restrains. Papa tiptoes into the room.

"It's too early to give up, Mira. Listen, I have a plan – I will make a portable *ballet barre* for you that can fit right here." Papa stretches his arms showing me an imaginary *barre* between my bed and a wardrobe.

Hesitantly nodding, I return my gaze to the window. Papa walks to my desk. His glance drops on the "Snow Queen" script.

"By the way, how did that go? Did you awe the class with your script?"

"It went well, I guess." I shrug, not sure of anything anymore. "The play is the only thing that still keeps me on the surface. Allachka offered her classroom in the evenings as a workshop to create the scenery. She also will call Larissa's parents and ask if she can help design and paint the sets." A few wrinkles run through Papa's forehead, and I realize he struggles to remember who Larissa is.

"She is the girl who fell in the middle of our Mazurka dance, remember? Her illness was caused by contamination from the Chernobyl explosion. She had to quit our Ballet Academy and enroll in the Art school." I pause, my thoughts returning to ballet. "Papa, the *barre* is a really great idea; could you also help me with some stretching exercises?"

Papa enthusiastically nods. "Sure, we can start tonight."

“No,” I shake my head. “I’m too exhausted, I just want to go to bed.”

Chapter 12: BRILLIANT PLAN

Every afternoon, right after *Practica* and before we even change from our dance attire, we rush directly to the Russian classroom. Often losing a track of time, we stay there until the late evening, consumed with set painting and reciting parts. Tonight is no different; the arrow on the clock just passed eight, yet we are far from being done. Suddenly, an unknown man opens the door. He doesn't say, "Hello" but comes right in, stops in front of the blackboard and peers into our faces. Everyone is startled by the man's invasive appearance. Allachka breaks an uncomfortable silence first.

"May I help you?" I sense annoyance mixed with concern in teacher's voice.

"No help needed. I already found who I am looking for," says the man.

I follow the direction of his glare. Max looks frozen, holding the tree cardboard with one hand and gripping the paint brush with the other. The boy and the man stare at each other. The silence is so absolute I think I hear several drops of paint from Max's brush flop to the floor.

Finally, Max sets his work down and walks towards the man. Watching him move, I can't believe the transformation; nothing remains of the hero-like confident Max. The boy seems even shorter standing in front of Dydia[21] Kolya, as he calls the man during their brief conversation. Then the man strides out of the room without a glance. Max returns to painting his tree.

"Is everything all right?" asks Allachka with even greater concern in her voice.

"Yes, my step-dad needed to see me," answers Max, dipping his brush into a bucket of green paint. Those are the last words we hear from him for the rest of the evening.

I never thought there was a place for fear in Max's personality. I also didn't know he lived with a step-dad. How many more things don't I know about Max? I kneel over a vast piece of painted blue paper which, together with Natasha, we layer with glue and then splatter with finely crushed multicolored Christmas balls. The slivers of the sparkly balls create an icy image on the painted paper and will be used as the backdrop of

---

[21] A word for a familiar male adult or an uncle.

the Snow Queen castle. Still consumed with thinking about the scene I just witnessed, I barely notice a sudden sharp pain in my pointing finger, and before I react there is blood on the blue paper. Allachka hurries to put a band aid over my cut. Natasha sighs and together we begin to apply another layer of blue over the future backdrop.

It is nine o'clock when Allachka finally persuades us to go home. We gather our belongings and walk into the hallway. Feeling an urge to say something comforting to Max, I get by his side.

"Max," I call his name and pause, not finding the right words to continue. "Your tree turned out really great." I cowardly change the subject.

"I guess it turned out okay, thanks to Larissa's help."

"Asking Larissa to come back and help us with scenery was another great idea of Allachka." I say to Max's back while he scatters down the stairs. I realize he isn't interested in keeping up the conversation and watch his figure disappear. I feel annoyed but then recall the scene with his step-dad. I realize I pitied Max tonight for the first time.

With New Year's Eve rapidly approaching, winter's holiday spirit is in the air. New Year is one of the major celebrations in the Soviet Union, and a favorite for children and grown-ups. The families begin collecting groceries months beforehand to have a full table of enjoyable dishes and desserts. Children hang candies and mandarins wrapped in foil on the freshly cut Christmas trees. Moms are busy making costumes of Snow Flakes, Bunnies, Squirrels, and Father Frost's Daughters "Snegurochkas" for the New Year presentations at schools.

At the Academy, all the classrooms are lushly decorated with handmade paper garlands and painted "Happy New Year!" banners. There is also a tall spruce tree in the lobby of the Academy's auditorium. It smells of winter forest and is densely decorated with ornaments, silver "rain" strings, and snow balls of white cotton.

For the last three weeks we've been practicing the play and this afternoon we gather at the auditorium's lobby waiting for the permission to enter the stage for our dress rehearsal. Finally, Allachka comes through the door accompanied by the janitor with a heavy bunch of keys dangling from his wrist. The janitor opens the double door and the impatient students rush inside the auditorium.

"Arthur, Gena and Slavik, quickly bring the furniture onstage for the first scene," calls Allachka. "Max, check the stage microphones and the sound levels."

The boys carry out the stand with a painted window; I marvel at the two hanging baskets with flowers depicted on the window's perch – it was Larissa's idea as well as her creation. In front of the window, the boys place a table and a couple of short stools. I bring a pair of my old black skates and put them in front of the fireplace. They are boy's skates, which I used to learn to ice skate when I was eight. In the play, they belong to the little boy Kay. In the first scene, Kay leaves his friend Gerda to go skating on the town's main square where he meets the Snow Queen, dares to hold on to her sled and is granted her fateful kiss.

When all the props are placed backstage, the microphones checked and the actors have taken their places, we begin the run-through. I watch from the front wing, holding the script in my hand in case someone needs help with their lines, although no script is needed – I memorized everyone's part long ago.

Unexpectedly, during the scene in the forest, Gerda's dialog with a Robber-Girl is interrupted by a voice of absolute power and authority.

"Stop the rehearsal," Principal Bogdanov commands from the dimness of the audience. He marches up the short staircase on the side of the stage. The expression on his face communicates he is not here to enjoy our play.

"Everyone, immediately line up on stage," he orders.

"That's a bad start," I think, and hurry to stand in line between Vita and Natasha.

"Something out of the ordinary has happened in our Academy." Principal scans each of our faces twice before he continues. "Someone in your class is responsible for taking a rifle from the Military

Preparedness classroom." He pauses again. "It would be naive for me to hope for the criminal to step forward right now." The word he chooses to describe one of my classmates sends a wave of chills throughout my body.

"Yet, I assure you that the truth will be revealed when each of you, one by one, stands on the rug in my office. No one will uphold and the criminal will be suspended with disgrace. Until then, the play is cancelled."

The Principal turns on his heels and disappears back into the darkness. While a minute ago I felt shivers, now I feel several drops of sweat making their way down my spine; I realize my dress's elegant top is glued to my back. I notice no one moves from the Principle's ordered line. Allachka ascends to the stage. Her face turned gray.

"Put away the scenery and meet me at my classroom." That's all she says and disappears through the lobby's door.

Slowly, the students begin to move again. I lift one of the trees and carry it backstage. Not paying attention where I step, I trip over a microphone cord and almost fall on top of Max. When I apologetically lift my eyes and look at him, expecting the usual sarcasm, I meet a face of a ghost. In an instant I somehow know who is the "criminal".

I get rid of the tree and squat next to Max, pretending to help him roll the microphone cord.

"Where is it?" I whisper.

His gaze is frightened, yet he surprises me with an immediate answer. "It's in Razdevalka, behind my locker."

"Are you insane?" I gasp, but my brain begins to search for a solution.

"Most likely Bogdanov will call the boys first. Maybe "The Amazing Four" can help," I whisper and leave his side.

Instead of following everyone upstairs to the classroom, I sneak out from the group and run down to the boys' Razdevalka. I search behind the locker's shelf and quickly spot the brown object. My hands shake; I bite my dry lips and taste blood in my mouth. Yet, I pull the rifle from behind the shelf and wrap it into the robe I slip off my shoulders. Now what, I think in panic, where do I take this monster? My glance falls on the window. At the very same time I hear voices in the hallway and without a second of hesitation, I push the window open and carefully place the wrapped rifle along the wall as far as possible from the window. Then I freeze, hiding between the window and the side of the shelves, while two boys from the upper grade enter the room and pass through into the one in the back. With lightning speed I dash into the hallway and don't stop running until I get to the fourth floor. Allachka meets me with a questioning look, yet she motions me to take the seat. Literally, a second later Bogdanov comes in and points at Gena who must follow the Principal to his office first. I shiver uncontrollably, either from missing my robe or from being scared, and Allachka notices.

"Mikhail Grigorevich," she catches the Principal just outside of the classroom, "could you permit the girls to be released so they can change from their costumes?"

Bogdanov hesitates for a second. His face is turned away from us, but I can read tension in his back and shoulders.

"The boys will be questioned first. The girls have my permission to change."

That's exactly what I need to complete my insanely dangerous rescue plan. On the way to the door, I pass Max's desk so closely my skirt gets stuck on uneven surface of its wooden side. I stop and carefully free the fabric. Everyone is silent and I don't dare say a word, yet I give Max a glance full of assurance.

"I have it." I whisper to Natasha as we come down the stairs and meet her horrified look. "It's Max." I press my lips to Natasha's ear. "He took it but I hid it for him outside the window." I realize I need more time to explain the situation to my bewildered friend.

Once changed, I wait for "The Amazing Four" to remain in Razdevalka and briefly tell them about Max and my plan to get rid of the weapon.

"I think we must take it some place where it will be found soon so everyone will be off the hook," suggests Tanya.

"You are right, but where?"

"Let's put it next to the concierge. She usually naps at this time of the day."

"But we can't risk carrying it through the building; it's too far and too dangerous."

"We won't need to do that. There is a door in the coat room that leads to the inner courtyard," replies Natasha.

"Perfect!" exclaim the rest of us.

Next, I choose the girl who has as much courage as the action needs. "Vita, you'll be in charge of the concierge. Let me know if she is asleep and if the grounds are clear. Natasha and Tanya, could you unlock the door and from there rush to the classroom? Allachka might notice our absence and get suspicious. Tell her that Vita and I are getting some bread from the cafeteria for everyone to snack on while we are waiting to be questioned."

I open the window and the cold surges all the way to my bones. I step up on the perch and squat to fit through the opening.

"See you at the front," I tell Vita. "And see you girls upstairs. Cover for us. Hopefully it'll work."

When I push myself over the window and land on the icy ground, I fully realize what kind of risk I'm putting myself through. The question "Why am I helping Max?" rushes through my head, but I have no time to think of the answer. Bent as low as I can and staying close to the wall, I creep around the building to the side of the boys' Razdevalka. I retrieve the object wrapped in my robe and, moving my feet as fast as I can in the hunched over position, I reach the coat room door.

The rest of the plan works the way we hoped it would. Already in the Russian classroom, chewing on rye bread we hear a loud hollering from the concierge who woke up and found the rifle standing next to her desk. I hold my breath, hoping that Max, who was called last and still hasn't returned from the office, didn't admit his crime.

I look at Allachka and see her eyebrows rise over the frame of her glasses; only for a brief moment she takes her eyes away from the page. She returns to reading the poem only to be interrupted by Max's return.

"The rifle has been returned and the Principal releases all of us for today, but he'll be holding a further investigation tomorrow." Max sounds surprisingly calm.

"Bastard," I think, "my scared heart almost ripped from nerves while saving his life." Everyone gathers their belongings and begins to leave.

As four of us turn from the Academy's alley into the dark path between the apartment buildings, I hear a hard breathing behind my shoulder. I stop abruptly and turn around.

"Thank you for saving my life." Max looks straight into my face. His eyes sparkle in the dull light of the street lamp; his expression is genuine and convincing. I expected his gratitude and even prepared a response, yet I find myself silently staring back at the boy. Natasha comes to my rescue.

"That's right. You are in our debt for the rest of your life."

"Whatever you need and want." Max bows elegantly, like he is on stage playing a knight. "My Ladies, are you in need of my escort tonight?" Such an actor, I think, and play along.

"No Sir, you are released from your duties this evening," I answer with a slight nod and turn away from him. While I hear girls' giggling, I let myself dissolve in a priceless contentment of the night that could've turned an absolute tragedy. Suddenly a question that has been spinning in my head all evening long pops out again.

I turn around and call out to Max. "Why did you take it? Why risk so much, for what purpose?"

"I needed it to stand my ground. I guess it was a stupid and reckless plan. I wanted to use the weapon to scare my step-dad." Max looks at his feet while he answers me. "Thanks again." He awkwardly waves and takes off, escaping any further questioning.

As I say good bye to my friends, stepping off the tram at my station, the turmoil of thoughts scatters through my brain. I think of Max and his relationship with his step-dad. I think of Larissa who seems to be very happy outside of the Ballet world. I think of the play and my role in putting it together, from the script to coaching the actors to playing one of the principle roles. My next thought hits me so unexpectedly I stumble and come to a halt just a few steps before the door to my apartment entrance: "Maybe Ballet doesn't have to be my only future." When I open the door and climb the stairs, I feel like a new me.

Chapter 13: "SNOW QUEEN"

On the day of the play I wake up long before the alarm, and by the time Papa comes to the kitchen, I'm dressed and have a pot of tea waiting for him on the table.

"What has caused this unusual morning behavior?"

"Papa, today is the day!" I exclaim. "We finally present our play to the entire school."

"That's right, I completely forgot." Papa scratches the top of his head. "It's a shame they don't allow parents in the Academy. You must promise to give me a detailed report on the entire event." He puts a skillet on the stove.

"Papochka, reports are your thing. How about I give you a review?"

"Review it is." Papa throws a piece of margarine on the skillet, which fizzes and pops until it is covered by the whisked eggs. Soon, the luscious smell of an omelet fills the kitchen. Papa and I sit down to breakfast with Niko helplessly watching the omelet disappear from our plates. His muzzle rests on top of the table, with his long snout pointing in the direction of my food.

Hurrying to finish, I let Niko fetch and gulp the last piece of omelet. Then I realize I might be late for school. "Papa, could you walk Niko for me, please?"

"Sure, Miss Playwright, but, since there are no more sets to paint, I hope you can walk your dog extra time this afternoon."

"I sure will," I answer, already in the hallway putting on my hat.

Papa and I go outside together. Niko pulls on the leash.

"Best of luck." Papa kisses my forehead and then gently pushes me towards the direction of the tram.

This morning at school none of my classmates cares about anything except the play. At first, Marina Stepanovna attempts to awaken our interest in graphs in her math class, but soon gives up and lets us chat about the upcoming event instead. As *Classica* begins, I find it very difficult to concentrate. Yet as we progress through the *barre*, I focus on the execution of the ballet steps and forget about the play. In the *center*, Violeta gives us a series of *pirouettes* as the second part of the *battement tendue*. Long before, my classmates and I came to a conclusion about “turning” versus “non-turning” days. There are days when you own the power to spin like a magic top - with ease and a minimum effort. Yet, on different days, no matter how much you think and visualize your body’s center, aligning the hip of the working leg over the instep and pulling up with all your strength, you still crash after a single *pirouette*. Luckily, today is my “turning” day and every time I complete a clean *double pirouette,* I peek at Violeta to see any sign of approval. Instead, she corrects or praises other girls. Although her neglect hurts my feelings, the satisfaction from the mastered movement fulfills my body. I imagine the day when I grow to become a professional dancer and will perform the *pirouettes en pointe* on the big stage, with only “turning” days on my calendar.

When the class is over and we dash down the stairs from the Ballet Gallery, I begin feeling nervous about the play. It’s not my part that worries me, but the whole event that I’m about to conduct. After getting changed into costume and making last minute arrangements, it's finally a show time. The auditorium is packed with students and faculty, the lights are dimmed and, as I hide in the first wing, I seem to hear audience breathing in unison. I motion to Max to pull on the curtain's string and slowly slide it open.

As introductory music fades away, Natasha and Slavik begin their first dialog. Everything runs smoothly. Now, it's my turn to appear on stage in the scene with Kay. I feel like royalty in my stunning gown designed and sewn by Babushka. The skirt of light blue chiffon touches the floor and moves with my every step as the waves of the ocean. The front of the blue silk bodice is embellished with a pattern of gold brocade and is trimmed with scattered sequins, imitation crystals, and pearls. The see-through sleeves of white gauze with angular ends create an image of icicles. So does the white collar attached to the dress's neck line, which extends all the way from the back of my shoulders to the middle of my head. A shiny crystal diadem crowns my head completing the outfit. Suddenly, I'm not shy of my height anymore; in fact, I stand even taller - proud of my stature and enjoy impersonating the character. In the corner of my brain, I keep wondering what an impact my appearance would make on Violeta and her attitude towards me.

When the Queen is defeated by the love and bravery of little Gerda, the play is over and the audience pours out of the auditorium and into the foyer to greet and compliment the actors. I feel like I'm floating in the air. Principle Bogdanov shakes my hand and congratulates me on the great production; a couple of the ballet teachers of the upper grades express their delight and admiration. Yet, my eyes keep searching for Violeta and finally meet hers. She finishes talking to Allachka and heads towards me.

"I'm impressed with the play and your involvement in it, Techenko." I listen for sarcastic tones in Violeta's voice but don't hear any.

"Obviously you have other talents, so why are you being so stubborn about ballet?"

My body stiffens and I clutch my skirt's fabric between my fingers. I feel assaulted by teacher's question. Not finding the courage to look into Violeta's cold grey eyes, I stare at my feet and answer.

"Because I love it the most. And I'm not about to quit on my dream to become a ballerina. I can still prove myself."

"Very well. We'll see about that." Somehow Violeta's offensive and doubtful words, instead of discouragement, sparkle a new fire of action inside of me. We have two weeks of winter vacation ahead and I know exactly the way I'm going to spend them.

Every day of the winter break, I force myself to work at the *ballet barre* in the morning, stretch before lunch and again with Papa later in the day, and go for a run in the evening. The days in January are very short. The sun sets around four and, since the light from the street lamps is scarce, and the snow melted after New Year, darkness prevails outside. Yet, it doesn't interfere with my running routine.

This afternoon, I leave the apartment later than usual. Niko almost lost his patience while I watched my favorite movie – it is my vacation after all! Now, finally outside, he eagerly pulls the leash and I feel my heart rate steadily rising while I try to keep up with my dog. Plastic bags are wrapped around my legs, covering by long underwear and thick pants on top. My legs quickly become steamy hot and heavy with sweat. That's the only way to thin my thighs without any sort of dieting, which both Papa and Babushka are strongly against.

Suddenly, Niko spots a cat and breaks into a chase. I struggle to keep up with the hound but have no other choice - his leash is wrapped around my wrist, cutting sharply into my skin. Unaware, I step on the edge of a big ditch, lose my balance and fall; at the same time I hear a loud crack and feel a sharp pain in my ankle. Plunging down, I hit my knee and roll into my side. My sudden fall and shouting brings Niko to an immediate halt. The dog sniffs me first and then begins to lick tears from my face. My foot hurts so much, I'm sure it's broken. My pants are ripped and skin on my knee is badly scraped, too. The apartment is not too far, but walking there on my own is impossible. I also realize I'm in one of the most remote parts of our courtyard and the chances of seeing a pedestrian are very slim.

"Niko, go get some help," I beg the dog. But he seems content as he lies on the ground, licking his paws, resting from the chase.

"Papochka, please find me," I beg into the darkness of the evening.

I keep occupied thinking of Mama's arrival at the beginning of July, the only happy place and time my imagination can take me now. Lost in my thoughts, I can't tell how long it's been since I left the apartment, but when Papa appears from around the corner and the way he charges towards me, I sense I was missing for a while, causing Papa great anxiety.

After a visit to the doctor, we learn the foot isn't broken yet my ankle is badly sprained, which causes swelling and pain. Numb with a disbelief, I listen to the doctor's verdict banning ballet classes for two months. After we leave the clinic, Papa delivers me back to the apartment. Since he spent the entire morning by my side, he must return to work and stay there late into the evening. Purposelessly, I limp around the apartment. I still manage to stretch, yet there is nothing else I can do; all the activities that seemed so desirable when I forced them aside to do my *ballet* routine, now don't appeal to me at all. Finally, I settle on the perch of my window with a book. Time stops as I submerge into the world of

Twenty Years Later by Dumas, and at first I don't even notice the phone is ringing. I hobble to the other room to pick it up, excitement and hope grow inside of me – I recognize in the phone's frequent ring the international call. The line crackles and fusses and then what seems from just across the street the beloved voice calls my name.

"Mirochka, dochen'ka, how are you?"

"Mama!" Is all I can say, and then a cascade of emotions sobs into the receiver.

"What's wrong, Mira, please, talk to me," Mama sounds so worried. I feel my heart break in half – what do I tell her?

"Mamochka, my foot hurts, really bad. I fell yesterday while running with Niko and sprained my ankle."

"My poor kitten," Mama's voice is filled with worry and pity. "How much I wish I could be there with you."

"Me too, Mama, but at least it's not broken and I'm still going to do my stretches and hope to come back to class even before the doctor told me I could."

"How is ballet? How are things with Violeta?"

That's the question I feared. What do I tell her?

"Everything is well in ballet, except I can't dance now. But, Mama I want to tell you about our play. Oh, and wait till you hear about Max and the story with the rifle."

"Rifle?" Even without seeing Mama's face, I can picture her eyes widen with surprise.

I get comfortable on the floor, propping a fat pillow behind my back hoping that Mama prepaid for at least an hour conversation.

Chapter 14: Women's Day

The night before classes resume, Papa phones Violeta and informs her about my ankle. She receives the news with indifference. While I must sit through all my dance classes, I'm not required to attend *Practica.* Therefore, every day I leave early and head home. On Friday night, Papa announces he has arranged for me to skip school tomorrow.

"Mama called me at work this morning with a wonderful idea for you to try the training program at the Gym of the Ukrainian National Gymnastics team while you recover. I stopped by the Gym today and spoke with their main coach. She remembers your Mom and agreed to have you come. Tomorrow morning, we need to be there by eight."

The following morning, an hour earlier than Academy's classes start, Papa pushes me, not fully awake and nervous, into a small hallway of the Gym. While Papa briefly exchanges greetings with the Gym's head coach, I peer through the door into the spacious area with a high, dome-shaped roof. Then I follow the coach's fit figure in the blue athletic suit to a tiny locker room, relieved to find it completely empty. It's warm and humid inside; the air smells of sweat and powder. Changed into the sweat pants over a ballet leotard, I'm given two small but heavy sand bags attached to the bands that must be worn around my ankles. Burdened with these weights, even walking is a challenge. Yet, I'm forced to lift and lower my legs numerous times, to execute splits and "scissors" in the air while lying on a thick mat, surrounded by shouting gymnastic coaches. With the next set of the exercises I'm allowed to stand. While stretching one leg up on the wall ladder, I'm finally able to observe what's happening around me. One gymnast repeatedly executes a series of complicated turns while twirling a stick with the ribbon above her head. Another student practices with two batons. She runs and jumps into a perfect split while throwing two batons above her head. While her apparatuses are still in the air, she lands, somersaults twice, and catches her props. Her coach is very loud. I feel uncomfortable listening to all the criticisms she spills on the girl. The student closest to me is standing on one leg while the coach pulls her other leg up on the side of her body, far past girl's ear. I hear her sobbing. These girls train like beasts - even in comparison to ballet students. I witness more sweat, tears and yelling than I've ever seen during our practices.

I sweat and endure for two hours, and when I'm finally liberated from the weights and tear off my heavy pants, I literally feel fitter and lighter.

"Thank you, Irina Victorovna," I wave to the coach.

"Will you be coming back?" she asks.

"Can I come every afternoon?" I ask in reply and receive the coach's nod; I turn around to leave, then abruptly come back to the door.

"Can I also come on Sundays?"

I spend every afternoon and weekends working out at the Gym. Busy with this new training routine, helps me get through the dark and cold winter months. Today, I finally enter the studio wearing my ballet attire instead of carrying a note book to record Violeta's corrections. I slip off my robe, put it on top of the radiator and freeze, catching a startling image staring at me from the big wall mirror. Surrounded by a circle of girls, I listen to their compliments when Violeta walks in.

"Welcome back, Techenko. I hope after taking such a prolonged vacation, you will triple your effort in class," she announces with her usual sarcasm.

Yet, I immediately catch Violeta's perplexed stare scanning my body from head to toe. Then the class begins. Forcing my feet into the turned out positions is the biggest challenge I face. The injured ankle feels weak and vulnerable. Yet, when we get to *adagio* at the *barre*, I hold my legs in high extensions with unexpected ease and don't show a sign of tremble or weakness. Next come *grand battements* and my legs fly up effortlessly. I take it easier during the *allegro* part of the class and only mark through *variations* during Practica.

Although in March, the days grow noticeably longer, it's still cold and wet, and the trees are lifelessly bare which makes this first month of spring hard to distinguish from winter. In the mornings, I still hide my nose deep inside my scarf. On my way to the tram station, I don't bother to avoid multiple puddles while listening to the thin layer of ice cracking under my boots. I pity the birds searching for food on top of the bare ground and feel nostalgic for warmer days. Yet, the thought of approaching celebration of Women's Day lightens up my spirits and warms my heart.

There are no religious, only Soviet holidays marked red on the calendar, and International Women's Day is one of them. On March 8, the entire country celebrates women by having this day free of work or school. The streets fill with men of all ages carrying flowers. The selection of flowers is scarce and bouquets are modest: mostly tulips, daffodils, snowdrops, or branches of mimosa. Still, it creates an unforgettable atmosphere of merriment and joy.

I await and prepare for the day before the actual Women's day, as it usually celebrated at the Academy. The night before, I sewed stitch by stitch a bright white lace onto the collar and cuffs of my school dress uniform. As I get ready for school this morning, I look in the mirror and feel dissatisfied: apparently I've outgrown my dress and the waistline now rises to the bottom of my ribcage revealing ugly wrinkles on the thick cotton tights that sag around my knees. I fetch a pair of colorful gaiters from my drawer and pull them over the tights.

"Much better," I tell Niko who follows my every move with his clever amber eyes, obviously impatient to be taken out on his morning walk. "I wish Mama was here to help me with my hair – she would braid it in such a pretty way for this special day." I keep talking to the dog. I sigh and pull my hair up in a ponytail, wishing I could just let it down, but this is not allowed at school.

At the Academy's lobby, I get the same sensation as before a performance. My heart uncontrollably races and my legs feel numb. I lower my school bag on the bench in Razdevalka, while Vita and Lena greet me from the perch of the window. Soon, Vera walks in.

"Do you think boys will do something special for us today?" She seems very excited and worried too.

"Remember, how all the girls got upset last year when only Natasha found a flower on top of her desk?" asks Vita.

"I think the boys should be forced to prepare better this time," suggests Lena.

"I don't like using force in order to get a simple flower. I wish it will be a gesture coming from their hearts." I say.

"Mira, you talk about boys as they were our equals. Yet, science proves they are a couple years behind in their social and physical development," proclaims Tanya who walks in, catching the last part of our discussion.

We all laugh and suddenly I feel at ease and not concerned about whether I will get any flowers today or not.

When we get to our math classroom, we find our desks covered with uniform-looking tulip bouquets of three. Obviously - a work of our home room teacher. Boring, I think, but at least no one feels left out and upset.

Before Classica, we put all the flowers into a glass jar borrowed from chemistry class. The tulips are all red, their petals held together with thin rubber bands. Heads down, bent on fragile stems - that's how I picture us, as we shuffle to the second floor of the gallery for our ballet class.

As Violeta walks in, she asks our pianist to hold the first cords. "I want to make an announcement to push everyone to work harder and more determined to overcome their flaws. The faculty made a decision to stage Chopiniana[22] for our annual Academy performance. The director himself will choose the best students from our class and from the level above to partake in this one act ballet." Violeta scans our faces, turns around and sits on the bench, crossing her legs. "Now back to work," she claps her hands and we hurry

[22] One act romantic ballet choreographed by Michel Fokine in 1907, also known as Les Sylphides.

to place our feet in a tight fifth position. We take a breath by opening both arms to the side and reverence.

After the class, as we walk towards the basement chattering about the new challenge of auditioning for Chopiniana, I catch a glimpse of a shadow-like figure sneakily hurrying away from the entrance of our Razdevalka. When I open my locker, a greeting card falls out. Lightning-fast I pick it up and stack back onto the shelf. Immediately, I hear Natasha's exclaim:

"Look what Mira got!"

"It's a box of chocolates!" announces Tanya.

Not sure how to react, I pick up the box sitting on top of my bag, pull the top open, and offer the chocolates to my friends. I never reveal the card but the wide rumor begins to circulate around Razdevalka: the gift is from Max. I hide the card in my bag and wait to read it at home. Max's writing is neat and the words are nice but they leave me feeling disappointed. Did I hope to see more than a simple "Max" at the bottom of the card?

I hear our front door and Papa comes in greeting me from the threshold. I show him the box.

"Why are the chocolates almost gone?" He questions me with a chuckle.

"I hope you don't think I ate them all myself. I shared them with the girls but now I feel guilty of not thinking of you and Babushka. I should be less selfish."

"You are the least selfish person I know." Papa confines me in his big arms. "But for bringing home an almost empty box of chocolate, you owe me peeling the potatoes for our supper."

Papa leaves my room, but then his head reappears from behind the door.

"I forgot to ask, who gave you those chocolates?"

"Max did, in a secret manner."

"That's what I thought. He is a nice guy."

"He is okay." I say and hope Papa goes to the kitchen and forgets about Max.

Chapter 15: COUNTRYSIDE

The strength in my ankle improves daily. Learning the parts from Chopiniana inspires and excites me. I find the absence of usual Violeta's attacks and embarrassing moments during Classica, encouraging. I'm not her favorite, but every class she grants me with several corrections and there is no sarcasm in her tone.

Focusing on Chopiniana helps me ignore the wintery weather that seems never to end. Finally, when April arrives it brings the thaw that everyone desperately awaits. On Saturday, after school, "The Amazing Four" takes a detour from our usual walk to the tram station and stops at the Dairy store.

"Mira, do you still go to that Gym?" asks Vera, while searching in her wallet for the five cents she lacks to pay for her drink.

"Only on Sundays now. Here, I've got ten." I give the change to the vendor.

"Violeta treats you like a new student since you came back from your injury!" exclaims Natasha.

"It's almost a miracle!" joins in Tanya, sipping the foamy milk shake from the glass.

"No miracles involved, I swear, only very hard and persistent work." I lick the cream foam from my upper lip, indulging the taste of my favorite drink I wouldn't allow myself to have for the past three months.

The four of us stand by the counter next to the open window. The gentle April breeze comes through, toys with our loose hair and makes us push it away from our faces too often. But no one seems to mind. I take a deep breath, fill my lungs with delicious fresh air and let my body soak in a moment of contentment. Briefly my thoughts leave the company of my friends and I dream about visiting our country house. Vera brings me back to our ballet life with her question.

"We've learned the entire Chopiniana and have been practicing it for a month now, when do you think the director will pick the main cast?" she asks.

"Didn't Violeta mention beginning of May?" replies Natasha. "I assume most students will be chosen from the grade above us."

"Auditioning next to them will be tough," sighs Vera.

Our glasses are almost empty. But before we take the final sip, Natasha suggests, "Let's raise our glasses for a successful audition!"

"And for the finally arrived spring! Look outside, you just can't help but be joyful when everything around comes to life," I add as our glasses blissfully clink.

During the following three weeks, the temperature rises every day. When the warm weather finally settles, it allows Papa and Babushka to plan a trip to our country house. On Tuesday evening, over our usual late dinner, Papa announces, "Mira, you'll have to miss the Gym this weekend."

"That's fine, I can miss it once. When would we leave?"

"Right after school on Saturday."

"Niko, we are going to our dacha!" I exclaim, jumping to my feet and lifting my dog's front legs off the floor. Niko is used to doing the "Happy dance" with me, trained since he was just a puppy; our dance routine usually resolves with him beginning to softly bite my hand to let me know when he needs his four legs back on the ground.

The rest of the week I count days and then the hours until the bell rings, releasing me from the last class on Saturday. Having my bag ready since lunch, I charge directly for the exit. There are only four cars in the parking lot. Niko's head is sticking out from our car window; his tail wagging wildly. He is as excited as I am. I jump into the back seat next to Niko as Papa presses on the gas. By the time we drive 140 kilometers on the two-lane road heading Southeast from the city, darkness wraps the village where our small cottage stands. I can't see our garden or the yard in front of the house; all that is left for me to do is to bring the fire wood for the adobe stove inside the cottage, to warm up the interior and get rid of the smell of winter and humidity. Soon, I go to bed and easily fall asleep with a crackling sound of fire underneath me while resting on a bed built on top of the fire place. Invented more than a century ago, such beds served as comfortable sleeping places in every cottage of the Ukrainian village.

Next morning, I get up with the sun. Soon Babushka will list the chores to be done around the cottage and the garden, so I hurry to escape. I run towards the river, feeling weightless on the sandy path. My feet easily bounce off its firm, slightly wet surface. I imagine how different it will look and feel a few months later, when I return to spend my summer vacation. The sun will dry up the sand, turning it into the fine powder: soft and fluffy. Imagining baring my feet into the flour-like sand and feeling its pleasant warmth brings longing for summer. I stop in the middle of the road, between the bank of the river and our property, and look back. The land around our cottage is encircled with tall acacia trees. Their branches are still bare and the white walls of the small house shine through. The cottage faces the meadow with no other houses close by. It looks almost solitary, but I love this solitude. Satisfied with no Babushka in sight, I continue walking toward the river. My lungs fill with spring air – it is rich and fresh, almost drinkable. Patches of fog rise from the wet ground and suddenly Niko appears from one of them. He looks like he is smiling, loving every second of being out here with me. Together we approach the main stream of the river; the same Dnieper river that runs through Kiev and stretches all the way to the Black Sea. It's not as wide here, yet exceptionally picturesque. In the summer its banks, some low, some high, are covered with tall grasses, wild flowers, variety of trees, and white sand. I peer at the horizon. The shapes of the trees outlined on the pale blue sky with a precision of black ink. I touch the water – it's still icy cold from melted snow. Even Niko barely dips his paws and takes only a few short licks from the stream.

"That's all right boy, you'll come back in a month and be swimming here." Niko wags in agreement. I must wait longer than that. I need to get through all the exams and the Annual performance before I get rewarded for all my hard work with summer vacation. I look at the sun, guessing what time of the morning it is, and decide it is time to head back and help around the property.

The rest of the day I spend raking and removing the old leaves and freshly cut branches that Papa keeps piling up for me. I also help Babushka with planting around our vegetable garden. My chores have doubled since last summer. After the Chernobyl explosion no one took care of the garden or the orchard. Three of us work all day, forgetting about the need to eat. Luckily, around five in the afternoon, one of the neighbors brings freshly caught and already fried fish that smells delicious and makes our stomachs growl. Babushka quickly spreads a floral plastic tablecloth on the outside wooden table, underneath the blooming apricot tree. A big plate filled with small fillets of river fish covered with layer of flour and then fried in sunflower oil. The coating is crunchy and the fish tastes soft and juicy. Boiled potatoes and young sprouts of garlic complete our dinner. We drink the well water, which Papa tested earlier for radiation. The multiple layers of sand inside the well serve as natural filtration system. It cleaned water and and Papa's test came back negative.

Tired and hungry, we eat in absolute silence with only the sound of bees buzzing and the birds sporadically screeching from the sky. After we clean up the table, Niko returns from whatever places in the village he visited. Breathing hard, with his tongue hanging over the side of his mouth, his long hair covered with grass, Niko begs for water. He drinks an entire bowl, jumps in the back of the car and sleeps for the next two hours while we finish a few more tasks and put away the gardening tools. When the enormous disk of the scarlet sun begins to roll towards the far meadow on the horizon, we reluctantly pack our scarce belongings and return to the city.

Chapter 16: NIKO

Monday brings the usual stress of a new week of chores and responsibilities. Several days pass until Papa and I simultaneously notice that Niko isn't himself. The dog barely touches his food, doesn't beg for ours, and lacks the energy to keep up with me during our evening jogs. On Thursday night, Niko refuses his food entirely. His nose feels dry and fiery hot. Papa is sure the dog is running a fever, and without delay drives Niko to the veterinarian. I stay behind to finish my homework, but soon realize I keep reading the same passage in my history textbook over and over without registering any facts in my head; all I can think about is what is wrong with Niko.

When I hear the key in the door, I jump up from the chair and rush to meet Papa and Niko.

"The vet found a tick. It transmitted Encephalitis into Niko's blood stream." Papa tiredly lowers himself onto a kitchen stool.

"But, Papa," I interrupt, "I checked for ticks right after we came back from dacha on Sunday evening, I always do!" I yell my last words defensively, yet already sense a dark cloud of guilt descending.

"I know you did, don't blame yourself. It took the vet a long time and a special light to locate the tick on Niko's neck. It was buried deep inside his long, thick hair."

"So, what will Encephalitis do to him?" I ask already sobbing.

"Mira, I don't see any reason to hide the truth from you: Encephalitis is a very serious condition which causes inflammation in the brain – we might lose Niko." Papa takes me by the shoulders but I twist in his arms and pull away from him. I run to my room, where Niko is lying quietly on the rug by my bed. I throw myself next to him on the floor.

“I’m so sorry, boy.” I spread my arm across my dog’s wide chest and kiss his hot nose. I hear the weak sound of his tail thump once on the floor; it’s obvious that even such a small movement is an immense effort for him. My crying grows into uncontrollable sobs. Papa kneels down next to us. I bury my face into Niko’s hair; my body quivers irrepressibly. I feel like screaming.

“Mirochka, listen to me, there is still hope. Hope dies last, remember?” I nod, remembering a year ago when Niko got lost and was missing for more than a day.

Papa gently places his hand on my head and continues, “The vet injected the initial dose of medicine and gave me the rest. The medicine is very strong and should kill the disease, but might damage Niko’s other organs. Yet, Niko is young and strong; if his body can sustain this medicine, he will live.”

I nod again, but the clump that seized my heart when I first heard about the tick seems to grow bigger and bigger; I can barely breathe and can't get rid of the thought of losing Niko.

I leave my sleeping dog and shuffle to the kitchen. There, I kneel in front of the small crucifix and stare at the bronze figure that Papa attached to the wooden strut for mainly decorative purpose. Both of my parents were raised as Atheists, encouraged by the anti-religious communist regime. I've only entered a church once or twice in my entire life. I barely know how to pray and only follow my natural instincts. Peering at the crucifix, my eyes hurt from tears, I whisper a desperate prayer, filled with promises, pleadings, demands, even threatening to the mighty power whose presence I feel now all around and within me.

The next day, at the Academy, it's impossible to think of anything except my beautiful hound. I tell my friends what happened to Niko and his diagnosis. During Classica, Violeta casually mentions that audition for Chopiniana will take place today during Practica. I barely care.

When we arrive at the door of the ballet studio, I realize I forgot my pointe shoes in Razdevalka. Prepared to face Violeta's anger for being late and at the same time feeling indifferent to her insults, I turn around.

"Here, I fetched your shoes for you." Natasha hands me the sack with my point shoes. "You are not yourself, Mira. Even during the worse times with Violeta, you always talk to us and crack jokes. This morning in Razdevalka you were absolutely silent; and there is this absent look on your face….. I wish there was something I could do to help." Natasha swiftly hugs me, takes my hand and pulls me into the studio. I catch a sight of Violeta's figure at the other end of the gallery.

Natasha's kindness provokes a turmoil of feelings in me. I want to leave the studio, leave the Academy building and run away to a place where I can let myself cry. But I can't. I must stay and dance. I must try to do my best *port de bras*, create long lines in my *arabesques*, and execute flawless jumps.

The audition begins with the upper grade joining us in the studio. I point my feet as hard as I can and force my legs to stay up in the air higher than ever. Sweat cascades down my forehead, lands on my eyelashes and drips down my cheeks. I feel it streaming down my spine. I wish the pain in my exhausted muscles would overcome the pain I feel inside when thinking of my sick dog. After we perform all the parts of the Corps de ballet, the director and Violeta leave the studio. I lower myself to the floor, away from my chatting friends, and wait. Violeta comes back with the cast list. I hardly pay attention while she reads the names. Yet, I clearly hear my name and Natasha's. Any other day I would burst with pride and exhilaration, yet there is no place for joy in my heart. Instead, a flood of tears rolls down my cheeks mixing with my sweat. When the teacher releases us for today, I clumsily curtsy and hurry towards Razdevalka, leaving my friends behind.

As we walk to the tram, Tanya, Vera and Natasha talk about the audition and its outcome.
I keep silent. I don't really care. I care of nothing except how fast I can get home to see Niko, to check if he ate and take his temperature. Then, hopefully, I can take him on a walk. This morning, he was so weak on his legs that Papa had to carry him up and down the stairs. Finally, the tram arrives at my stop.

"I will walk with you," says Natasha following me down from the tram's steps.

"Thank you, but you better not. I must run. Niko has been home alone all day." The pedestrian light changes to green before I hear Natasha's reply. I dash towards the intersection and all the way across the street. I don't stop running till I get to the building's door. Then, I run up the stairs. I'm surprised and happy to see Papa at home. He is busy over the stove. I pull off my shoes and tiptoe into my room. I find Niko there, sleeping on a thick blanket on the floor. I caress his long silky coat. Papa enters the room.

"Why are you home so early?" I question him.

"Babushka was here at noon. She came to help with dinner and when she saw Niko phoned me at work. Niko's condition has worsened; she wanted to take him outside, but he wouldn't get up. The infection is still spreading. He even had a few seizures. The virus affects the nervous system, so I warn you not to get scared if he does something unusual; like begins spinning in a circle or drops his head involuntarily. Those are all the normal signs…."

"Normal?" I interrupt, not able to handle these horrific facts. "You can't call it normal, don't pretend it is normal!"

"What do you want me to do, Mira? Babushka cried in this very chair just half an hour ago. Now you are yelling like it is my fault Niko is sick. I just try to stay calm and reasonable. I still need to run this family until Mama comes back from China."

The reminder of Mama and our decision to keep Niko's illness a secret from her, pulls the last string. Like a bullet, I charge out of the room, slip on my old running shoes and shut the door behind me. I run and run, wanting to get lost in this dark and foggy April evening. I realize I'm trying to escape from nothing and no one. Tired and thirsty, I knock on my door, finally able to accept reality. I feel older and ready to share the responsibilities of taking care of Niko with Papa.

Over the next two weeks, we follow the schedule of the medicine and injections. Several times, Papa drives Niko to the vet for the blood tests. At the Academy, interacting with my friends and practicing Chopiniana helps get me through my day. At home, in the evenings, I try my best to block any thoughts of losing my dog by adding an extra load to my after-school stretching routine. Every night, before I go to bed, I light a candle next to the crucifix and say my "homemade" prayers. During one such prayers, I think of going to church.

Without delay, I decide to implement my thought the very next day. After *Practica*, I take a tram with Vera and Tanya in the opposite direction of my home, telling the girls I must go to the vet's clinic to get Niko's medicine. I hide the real destination of my trip because attending a church could be justified for an old babushka, but not for someone who wears a red Pioneer scarf and represents a Lenin[23] follower; if someone finds out, my action could be considered shameful and might jeopardize my future in Komsomol[24].

I run down the stairs that lead to the entrance of the subway station, loosen my scarf, pull it off my neck and hide it inside my school bag. The subway's direct line takes me to the University station, which is located

---

[23] A founder of the Russian Communist Party.
[24] Leninist Young Communist League.

near the main building of the Kiev State University, but even closer to St. Vladimir's Cathedral – one of the few churches in Kiev that fully operates and holds daily services.

As I approach the Cathedral's main entrance, I raise my head and peer at the image of Jesus on top of the church's arched door. Incidentally, the bells on the main dome begin to chime; awkwardly I cross myself and enter the church. Immediately the sacred dimness of the candle-lights and the strong smell of incense transform me into a different world. I don't dare to walk down the main aisle, instead take stealthy steps along the side of the building. The beauty and the color of the interior for a moment force me to forget the reason for my visit. As I slowly walk down the side aisle, I admire the vast mosaics that embellish every wall, every corner and the entire ceiling of the church. I stop several times to marvel at the images of the Saints and the significant religious scenes all embraced in the mosaic frames, masterly crafted of small colorful stones. On the far end of the cathedral, I see the Iconostasis[25]. Magnificent, it

---

[25] A wall of icons and religious paintings that separate the nave

towers over everything and everyone in its white marble and gold beauty. It seems lit from within by some magical light. Next to the Altar, I pause physically feeling a stare from the main Cathedral's fresco, The Holy Mother of God. Only when I notice the pain in my knees, do I realize I've been kneeling on the hard marble floor in front of the Iconostasis. I guess I was sobbing too, because next I see a figure in a black nun's cloak bending over me.

"Little girl, are you mourning for someone in your family?" The voice is sweet and comforting. I want to answer this kind lady, but choke on tears. She kneels next to me and I hear her praying too. She reminds me of the nun that watched over Constance from "Three Musketeers", yet didn't save her from the evil Milady. Would she help me save Niko?

"My dog is like a brother to me, he is very, very sick," I manage to say.

"Oh, good." Good? I feel totally confused by her comment, but then she continues. "Your dog is still alive, I thought you lost someone. "Come." She gently

---

from the sanctuary in a church.

pulls me up by my elbow. "I'll show you the icon where you light the candle and ask for your dog's recovery."

I follow the nun to the opposite side of the church's nave; somehow feeling she's been sent to me from above. I light a candle and place it among others on top of the circular candle stand. I remain standing there for a while, staring at the representation of Saint Panteleimon[26] in silent prayer. Waiting and hoping is all I have left.

---

[26] Was a physician who dedicated his life to the suffering and the sick.

Chapter 17: HARD DECISION

"Incredible! Simply incredible! For the last two weeks, this dog's life was draining out of his body, yet he has what is called a 'second wind'. In all my years of practice, I've only read but never witnessed such a case." The veterinarian raises his eyes from the paper with Niko's blood test results. I shout with relief when I hear this announcement, and the next second realize my arms are wrapped tightly around the doctor's neck.

"I really thought you were going to choke that poor fellow." Papa chuckles as we step out of the clinic. Niko eagerly pulls on the leash excited by the unfamiliar smells of the new neighborhood.

The air smells of apple blossoms, and I fill my lungs with its delicious aroma. Happiness fills my entire being. I smile at the passing strangers and feel in love with the whole world. I raise my eyes up to the turquoise sky and whisper my thanks to the heavens.

"Papa, let's walk home," I suggest.

"But we are on the other side of the city. It will take us forever to get home," Papa argues.

"Forever is good. I want to enjoy this beautiful day, and I'm sure Niko does as well, right boy?"

Hearing his name, the dog turns his head and, I swear, I see him gaily nodding in total agreement.

I wrap my left arm around Papa's, my right hand strongly holds the leash and we begin walking. On our way home, we chose smaller streets with less traffic and cross multiple parks. I marvel at the newborn foliage that bravely exposes its bright green and still vulnerable surfaces to the world. New life, a new beginning, I think. I sense something new might happen to me. Deep in my thoughts, I suddenly notice our walk brings us atop the hill to The October Palace - one of the Kiev's main performing arts centers. From the Palace's front terrace, a large view of the city opens for our observation. The main square is in the center surrounded by red marble fountains and spacious sidewalks. Massive buildings of the Stalin[27] era, including the Central Post Office and the Trade-Union House, embrace the square, with the main street Khreschatyk cutting through, three lanes on both sides. A massive

---

[27] A leader of the Soviet Union from the 1922 until 1953.

monument built to honor the 60th anniversary of the October Revolution oversees the square; behind it an eye-catching view of the green hill topped with the Hotel Ukraina.

As we begin our descent, Papa points towards one of the three steep streets across the square that rises seemingly all the way to the sky, and asks. “Are you sure you can conquer that climb?”

“Absolutely. We only had *Classica* today and it’s my day off tomorrow.”

Papa catches my gaze. “So, things have improved with Violeta, haven’t they?” he asks.

“A hundred percent. Okay, maybe eighty, but I feel so different in class now. I don’t worry about being suspended from the Academy anymore and look forward to performing in Chopiniana.”

Papa looks at me fondly gently squeezing my hand. “And I look forward to seeing you dance. When is the Annual performance?” he asks.

"At the beginning of June. I'm so excited and nervous. It will be the first serious test to take a part in the ballet presented at the Academy's Annual performance. Not just to appear in a single dance with the students of my level, but to share the stage with the Academy seniors." I explain the importance of the event to Papa. "We even got measured for the romantic tutus that will be made at the factory of the Opera House especially for us." I half close my eyes under a pleasant afternoon sun and dream of the week of dress rehearsals and the night of the performance. Even there are numerous hours of tough and exhausting rehearsals proceeding that day, I feel a joyful anticipation.

"Papochka, enough discussion about ballet. Let's talk about the summer, about going to Moscow and how we will meet Mama at the train station. Do you know it will take five days for her train to get from Beijing to Moscow?" We make plans the rest of our way home.

I can't wait for the weekend to end and for Monday morning finally to come. The day is gloomy; warm but grey due to the overnight showers. More is expected, so I put on a rain coat and grab an umbrella.

Fog hangs on top of the city, making the end of my street disappear into unknown. I wonder if the red and yellow tram stop is still where it was yesterday.

When I get to Razdevalka, I immediately tell Vita and Lena about Niko. They share this happy news with everyone and each girl rushes to give me a tight hug expressing her sincere relief and joy.

During math, a rumor begins circulating around the classroom, migrating from one desk to the next, finally landing on the last row where "The Amazing Four" resides.

"A producer from a movie studio is here today. They are looking for a girl our age who can dance," Natasha whispers to me without taking her eyes from her work sheet.

"That's exciting," I answer, trying to sound as careless as possible while my heart triples its beat.

A real movie producer! Here, at the Academy! The thought doesn't leave me alone. I struggle to focus on the numbers until the bell rings. I try to focus on the definitions during biology class, until Natasha leans from her chair and whispers into my ear a question that wakes up an entire flock of butterflies in my stomach.

"Do you think they will come during our regular classes or during *Classica*?"

"Maybe both," I answer, "they might visit our parallel grade first though."

No one interrupts the rest of the biology lesson and after the bell, we rush to Razdevalka and then to the Ballet Gallery.

Vera volunteers to be on the watch for the movie delegation. The rest of us gather in front of the mirror, checking and fixing our hairdos, leotards and ballet slippers.

"They are coming!" Vera blasts into the studio, almost tripping over the watering can. We hurry to our places and freeze along the *barres* in awkward stillness.

A moment later, headed by Violeta, a group of two men and a woman walk in. Violeta offers the visitors a seat on the bench. Then, she overlooks the class and, seemingly satisfied with our preparedness, motions to the pianist. The pianist strikes the first chords and the class begins with our usual *reverence*. By the time we execute *rond de jambs par terre*, I feel emotionally drained and wish for the group to leave already. We turn to repeat the exercise on the left side. I'm relieved to be facing away from our guests. Suddenly, I feel someone's touch on my shoulder and turn my head to see Violeta. Without saying a word or stopping an exercise, she takes my hand and leads me towards the group on the bench.

"This is our Miroslava." Bewildered by hearing Violeta call me by my first name, I curtsy in front of the group. "She is a very smart girl and an "A" student in all her school disciplines." My bewilderment grows to a shock.

Next, a bold man in a distinguished colorful vest asks me a question. But instead of giving him a proper answer, I'm still processing what just happened to my ballet teacher. Luckily instead of thinking I'm deaf and dumb, they blame my silence on the music.

"The music is loud. Also, we don't want to further interfere with your class; would you mind, Violeta Yurievna, if we take Miroslava out in the hallway and ask her a few questions there?" asks a woman with a big photo camera hanging on her neck.

"Please, go ahead. You can keep Mira as long as you need her." Violeta's arm is wrapped around my shoulder as she guides me towards the door. I glance at my classmates and read a mix of surprise and envy in their looks. I look down, feeling uncomfortable, and step into the hallway. Relax and focus, I tell myself, sensing that something life changing is about to happen.

Every day now I wait for the news from the movie studio. On the day when I finally forget about it, we have a surprise visitor during biology. A young man accompanied by Principle's assistant enters the classroom. He looks unfamiliar but somehow I know he is a "movie person". My heartbeat triples. Natasha and I exchange glances.

"Miroslava Techenko," why his voice is so squeaky, that's the least I expected from a man of his stature and appearance. "Could you please come up front?"

I get up and almost trip over my bag on the floor. Feeling embarrassed by my clumsiness I approach the teacher's desk.

"Congratulations, you were selected to play Alena in "Before the Sunrise". Here is a paper with two numbers and names next to them that your parents need to call as soon as possible." I take the paper and hurriedly return to my seat supervised by stares from my classmates.

At home I deliver the message to Papa and hand him the paper with numbers. He heads towards the phone as I escape to my room. In a little while, Papa appears on its threshold. His face beaming with pride and satisfaction.

"Four weeks leave at the end of May for a movie shoot outside of Kiev!" Papa turns the chair away from my desk and sits down. "There are still some formalities we need to go through before I sign the contract. They expect both of us tomorrow afternoon at the main office of the film studio." Papa's voice is full of excitement. "I also need to confirm with Babushka that she can take a leave of absence and travel with you." He pauses and intently looks at me. “I seem to be more excited than you Mira, what’s the matter?”

“Papa, this movie shoot will force me to stop my ballet routine, not for a few days here and there, but for the entire month. In addition, I won’t be performing in Chopiniana!”

“Yes, I know, but isn’t this something you always wanted to try, especially after the success of your play? You have an opportunity to act and be a part of a real movie production! Not one audience a night, but thousands of people will see you on the screen.”

“The part I got is not the main role in the movie. It’s not such a big deal after all.”

Papa sits next to me on my bed.

“Mirochka, the choice is yours. I know it isn’t an easy decision to make. If you want, I can arrange a phone call with Mama.” I silently nod. Why it’s always so complicated? I wanted to act in this movie so much, but didn’t expect I would have to choose between this role and Chopiniana. A few months back, I thought of acting as an alternative to ballet. Does getting this role mean I push ballet aside?

After changing into my night gown, I sit on top of my bed hugging my knees. I point my feet very hard, so only the very tips of my toes are touching the bed spread. Then I relax the tight muscles. How many times have I done this exercise and many others to improve my arches? Endless times - through pain, through occasional laziness, despite any excuses my tired body came up with. The wind is playing with the curtain on the corner of the open fortochka. The room is filled with the early May air, which smells of young grass and the blossoms of the poplars. The bright green, caterpillar looking, blossoms are everywhere. Every morning the janitor mercilessly sweeps them away, yet by evening there are hundreds of them covering the courtyard surface, fallen on top of random cars, children's swings and slides. I feel sleepy. My eyes begin to close and my head falls on my knees. But the questions still spin in my brain: what if I like acting more than ballet? Would it change my future? Why can't this movie shoot take place in the summer instead of tearing me away from ballet now?

Several days later, when my entire class knows I would leave for a month long movie shoot, a long distance ring breaks our apartment's silence and sends me charging away from the open suitcase to the phone's receiver. I rush to pick it up and hear Mama's voice on the other end.

"Dochen'ka, Papa called me from work and briefly explained your dilemma."

"Mamochka, I'm so glad you called! What do you think?"

"First of all - congratulations on the role; that's wonderful news and I'm so happy and proud of you!"

"Mama, but do you think it's also a sign for me to choose acting over ballet? Now, when everything finally is going so well in ballet class! Even Violeta has changed; I proved to her I have a right to continue at the Academy. And what do I do now? If I choose filming, I will miss the annual performance and won't perform in Chopiniana and all my hard work, all my skipped weekends spent at the Gym, my sweat and my tears during the after-school runs and extra stretching, all will be wasted!"

"Hard work and its results never get wasted. I understand your dilemma; your chosen profession is extremely fragile - even one missed day sets you back in class. Ballet is your longtime dream, which you didn't give up even facing the harshest challenges. My advice to you will be to follow your heart." There is a sudden cracking on the line. I keep calling Mama's name yet only hear a deafening silence in respond. I drop the receiver and return to my room. I settle on my bed next to the suitcase, my gaze slides over the furniture, stopping on top of the chair where my ballet slippers await to be mended, then continues to the open window. "Follow my heart," I think out loud, "that shouldn't be too difficult."

It's Friday morning, the morning when a long distance train should carry me away from Kiev in the direction of the city where the movie shoot takes place. Instead, a rolling tram carries me through the familiar streets of my city. After I step out at my stop, I routinely wait for the tram from the opposite direction to see if any of my friends will arrive. In a few minutes though, I change my mind, deciding to walk on my own and, instead of following the usual path, I take a detour making a big loop through the park.

When I reach the Academy, I hide behind a massive tree and watch the students entering the building, keeping an eye on the time. Just as the bell is about to ring, I rush through the Academy's door and up the stairs to the Ukrainian language classroom. I peek inside. Satisfied the entire class is gathered, I finally reveal myself. As I casually walk in, I face a sudden silence. I glance at the faces of my friends and grin at the expressions of their sincere surprise and disbelief.

"What are you doing here?" Tanya is the first one to vocalize their questioning looks.

"I'm here to dance. Did you really think I would exchange the annual performance for some random movie shoot?" No one answers my question, yet multiple arms hug me all at once; squeezed and squashed in this friendship cluster, I feel joyful and confident I made the right choice.

Chapter 18: BEST SURPRISE EVER

It is finally the Academy's annual performance at the Opera House. Once again we enjoy the luxurious interior of the red velvet theater and indulge in the comfort of our dressing room. Yet, this comfort doesn't calm my growing nervousness; I'm one of the dancers in Chopiniana.

I finish applying my makeup and check the hair piece. Remembering mom's expression - "pin it to your brain", I grin and shake my head vigorously, making sure the delicate wreath that crowns my head could only come off if it pulls my brain with it. The makeup lady, shadow-like, slides into our dressing room and with embarrassment in her voice passes me Violeta's order to glue my ears.

"Sure, go ahead," I reply with an ease that surprises even myself.

"Does it hurt? I mean your skin from the glue?" Natasha asks empathetically.

"Not at all; honestly, I can't feel a thing." I answer while the lady applies the glue.

When my ears pressed to my head with a familiar white band, I pull on a pair of thick socks over my ballet shoes. I stand up and grab my pointe shoes, then catch a questioning glance from the rest of the girls. "Anyone wants to come upstairs to the studio with me? We can warm-up and mark our parts." All seven pairs of hands fly up.

Keeping my mind set on a warm-up instead of imagining a big stage and hundreds of eyes registering our every movement, gesture and facial expression, helps me calm down and regain control over my body. When we find ourselves in the dimness of the backstage, I feel slightly tired from our practicing, but also much more confident. I join the girls surrounding a wooden box with rosin. We pull down the back of our point shoes and dip our heels into the whitish, pine-smelling residue. Now, the shoes won't slip off our feet. Everything must be checked and secured; everything must be perfect.

Suddenly, like a thunder in the middle of a peaceful evening, a voice from the loudspeaker breaks my calmness, calling for the dancers to take their places on stage. I mechanically touch the wreath on my head, making sure it's secured and placed well, and walk on stage behind the closed curtain. My extremities begin shaking and my heart races again. Taking my place among other dancers, I imagine Papa and Babushka on the other side of the massive curtain. Then I think of Mama, looking beautiful in the evening dress she would wear for this special occasion, and imagine her secret "Good luck" wave from the first row of the audience. The tension in my muscles evaporates as I visualize waving back. At the same time, the curtain gradually begins to ascend, the tranquil sounds of Chopin fill the stage transporting me to a different world. I hold a pose with the other nineteen dancers on stage, picturing myself as a part of the vast Nineteenth century tapestry. My right arm is bent at the elbow and my pointing finger almost touches my chin. My torso leans towards the bent arm with my tilted head atop. I'm so focused on my stillness, I almost stop breathing. I know my musical cue by heart and begin my *port de bras* with other nineteen pairs of arms moving and breathing on stage as a whole. The magical power of the tiny fairy wings, attached to the waist of my dress, seem to hoist me from the ground when I rise on pointe. Soundlessly, creating an impression that our bodies are as light as an air itself, we *bourrée* across the stage, moving our feet in a serious of small very quick steps. Our tulle dresses flow in the air, forming picturesque patterns in front of the audience. Still, not a sound is produced by our feet. A team of teachers that prepared this piece tested our point shoes prior to the dress rehearsal. They made sure that while being hard enough to support us on *relevé*, the boxes of our shoes are soft and won't bang against the stage's wooden floor. The soloists begin their variations and I follow their every step and gesture, dreaming to appear in a solo at my graduation performance someday. A coda, the final part of the ballet, is my favorite to dance. It starts as a Mazurka, then switches to a Waltz, slows down almost to an Adagio and returns with a sudden energizing Mazurka rhythm. I try to make every *sissonne* perfectly light and every *attitude* complete with a curved line of my foot in the air. The dance formations constantly change: we travel in diagonals, create circles, and briefly stop and pose to highlight soloists' appearances. During rehearsals, the intensity of coda would steal my breath, yet now I feel I can and want to continue dancing through the night, with no worries of running out of energy. The only concern is the performance will end sooner than I want.

The moment the show ends and the curtain drops, I feel an incredible sadness. I hesitate to change from my tutu and meet my family outside the dancer's entrance. I'm glad to hear we must remain on stage while the Artistic director of the Opera House's Ballet troupe congratulates Academy's seniors. Following his speech, the assistant says a word.

"As you might know, every summer half of our Ballet troupe leaves on tour to Japan." I try to remain attentive and still, in spite of my exhaustion. Why do we need to know about the troupe's plans for the summer? Instead of curiosity, I feel the pain in my toes squeezed inside of the point shoes. "The remaining troupe will perform Swan Lake as a part of the July repertoire. This large production calls for numerous dancers. Therefore, we have chosen several Academy students to fill in for the missing Corps de Ballet."

I forget all about my aching toes and only hear my heart thump against my ribcage. I stare at the Artistic director who hands a piece of paper to his assistant. The man clears his throat in a serious of loud coughs and reads from the list.

"Irina Shumskaya, Svetlana Levko, Nataliya Shevchenko, Elena Trushko, Nina Rodnina, Miroslava Techenko." I hear my name clearly, yet still wonder if it's a dream or my imagination. Natasha proves it's a reality by squeezing my hand in a painful grasp.

"They called us! We'll be dancing with the Opera House's Ballet troupe in Swan Lake together!" Jumping in exhilaration, Natasha chokes on her last words.

"That's really superb news!" I finally feel relaxed and am bursting with happiness too. I seize Natasha's other hand and begin jumping with her.

Someone gently taps my shoulder. I turn around to meet Max's confident stare.

"Guess what I'm going to do in the Swan Lake?"

"Dance the main black swan!" I giggle.

"Silly girl. One day, I will be dancing a part of the Swans' guardian, Rothbard, but not this time." Natasha and I exchange looks. "My uncle is a stage director. He'll let me help with lights while the half of the stagehands crew is away on the tour. I also hope to talk him into bringing my buddy Gena along. Isn't that great?"

"It's not great, it's ten times greater than great!" Exclaims Natasha and I catch a sign of flirting in her voice. That amuses me; as well as the news about Max who will be around even in July when the school is out. But the revelation that comes to my mind next makes the best news of all: Mama will be back from Beijing just in time to see me perform in Swan Lake, as the most awesome "Welcome Back" surprise ever!

AUTHOR'S NOTE

About eight years ago, a thick stack of letters got in my hands. Fourteen year-old me wrote to Mom while she was working in Beijing. Scanning through pages, I read about hardships and misfortunes that had me sob. Yet, almost every episode from my school life had a heart-warming feel of promise and hope.

Within the following years I retold many of the stories to my ballet pupils while wishing I could organize them in a story line. However, I didn't want to write a memoire. And that's how Miroslava came to life. A fictional character who possessed some of my qualities and strived for my dreams, but also had fixed my mistakes and fulfilled the gaps I regretted.

Kiev Choreographic School (Academy) in the 90's

Ballet Sudio - with wooden floors and multiple radiator pipes (unfortunatey, they could not warm up the studio in the winter)

A dress that my babushka made when I was ten and later it was remade into a "Snow Queen" gown when I was fourteen.

Every daycare, every school and university, every office and manufacturing plant had multiple portraits of the USSR leader – Vladimir Lenin

Academy's stage where performances, dance examinations and patriotic events took place.

Main ballet studio in Kiev Opera House.

Kiev Opera House, a view on the audience from stage.
Photo courtesy of Nobuhiro Terada.

Made in the USA
Middletown, DE
27 October 2020